PENGUIN CLASSICS SCIENCE FICTION

Dimension of Miracles

Robert Sheckley (1928–2005) was born in New York City and raised in New Jersey. He joined the army and served in Korea from 1946–8, where, he said, he worked as '38th parallel guard, assistant newspaper editor, contracts and payroll clerk and, finally, guitarist in an army dance band'. On returning home to New York, he gained a degree and took a job in an aircraft factory, which he gave up on selling his first story to a magazine. His work appeared regularly in science-fiction magazines such as *Galaxy*, *Fantastic* and *Astounding Science Fiction* throughout the 1950s and 60s. In 1965, the story 'Seventh Victim', from his debut collection *Untouched by Human Hands*, was made into the cult classic film *The 10th Victim*, starring Marcello Mastroianni and Ursula Andress. In total, Sheckley wrote more than fifteen novels and four hundred short stories. In 2001, he was made Author Emeritus by the Science Fiction and Fantasy Writers of America.

T0368871

Dimension of Miracles

ROBERT SHECKLEY

PENGUIN BOOKS

PENGUIN CLASSICS

UK | USA | Canada | Ireland | Australia
India | New Zealand | South Africa

Penguin Classics is part of the Penguin Random House
group of companies whose addresses can be found at
global.penguinrandomhouse.com.

First published in the United States of America by Dell Books 1968
First published in Great Britain by Victor Gollancz Ltd 1969
First published in Penguin Classics Science Fiction 2020
002

Set in 11/13 pt Dante MT Std
Typeset by Integra Software Services Pvt. Ltd, Pondicherry
Printed in Great Britain by Clays Ltd, Elcograf S.p.A.

A CIP catalogue record for this book is available
from the British Library

ISBN: 978-0-241-47249-1

For my sister, Joan

Ah, I cast indeed my net into their sea,
and meant to catch good fish; but always I did draw
up the head of some ancient God.

Nietzsche

Part One

The Departure from Earth

Chapter 1

It had been a typically unsatisfactory day. Carmody had gone to the office, flirted mildly with Miss Gibbon, disagreed respectfully with Mr Wainbock, and spent fifteen minutes with Mr Blackwell, discussing the outlook for the football Giants. Towards the end of the day he had argued with Mr Seidlitz – argued vehemently and with a total lack of knowledge – about the steady depletion of the country's natural resources, and the remorseless advance of destructive agencies such as Con Ed, the Army Engineering Corps, tourists, fire ants, and pulp-paper manufacturers. All of these, he contended, were responsible in varying degrees for the spoliation of the landscape and the steady obliteration of the remaining pockets of natural loveliness.

'Well, Tom,' sardonic, ulcerated Seidlitz had said, 'you've really thought about this, haven't you?'

He hadn't!

Miss Gibbon, an attractive young lady without much chin, had said, 'Oh, Mr Carmody, I really don't think you should say that.'

What had he said, and why shouldn't he say it? Carmody couldn't remember, and thus remained unrepentant, though vaguely guilty.

His superior, plump, mild Mr Wainbock, had said, 'There really may be something in what you say, Tom. I'll look into it.'

Carmody was aware that there was very little in what he had said, and that it didn't bear looking into.

Tall, sardonic George Blackwell, who could speak without moving his upper lip, had said, 'I think you're right, Carmody, I really do. If they switch Voss from free safety to strongside cornerback, we'll *really* see a pass rush.'

Upon further reflection, Carmody decided that it wouldn't make any difference.

Carmody was a quiet man, of a predominantly melancholic humour, with a face that neatly matched the elegiac contours of his disposition. He was somewhat above the average in height and self-deprecation. His posture was bad, but his intentions were good. He had a talent for depression. He was cyclothymic – tall, beagle-eyed men of vaguely Irish antecedents usually are, especially after the age of thirty.

He played a decent game of bridge, even though he tended to undervalue his hands. Nominally he was an atheist, but more by rote than conviction. His avatars, which can be viewed in the Hall of Potentialities, were uniformly heroic. He was a Virgo, dominated by Saturn when it was in the House of the Sun. This alone could have made him outstanding. He shared the common human hallmark: he was simultaneously predictable and unfathomable – a routine miracle.

He left the office at 5:45 and caught the subway uptown. There he was pushed and jostled by many people whom he wished to think of as underprivileged, but whom he suspected of being acutely and irrevocably undesirable.

He emerged at 96th Street station and walked the few blocks to his apartment on West End Avenue. The doorman greeted him cheerfully and the lift operator gave him a friendly nod. He unlocked his apartment door, went in and lay down on the couch. His wife was vacationing in Miami; therefore, with impunity he propped his feet on the nearby marble table.

A moment later there was a clap of thunder and a flash of lightning from the middle of the living room Carmody sat upright and clutched at his throat for no particular reason. The thunder rumbled for several seconds, then was replaced by a paean of trumpets. Carmody hastily removed his feet from the marble table. The trumpets ceased, and were replaced by a brave skirling of bagpipes. There was another flash of lightning, and a man appeared in the middle of the brilliance.

The man was of medium height, stocky, had curly blond hair and wore a golden-coloured cloak and orange leggings. His features appeared normal except that he had no ears. He took two steps forward, stopped, reached into the empty air and plucked forth a scroll, tearing it badly as he did so. He cleared his throat – a sound like a ball bearing failing under a combination of weight and friction – and said, 'Greetings!'

Carmody did not reply, being struck by a temporary hysterical muteness.

'We are come,' the stranger said, 'as the fortuitous respondent of an ineffable desire. Yours! Do any men? No so, then! Shall it?'

The stranger waited for a reply. Carmody convinced himself by several proofs known only to himself that what was happening to him was indeed happening to him, and replied on a reality level:

'What in God's name is this all about?'

The stranger said, still smiling: 'It is for you, Car-Mo-Dee! Out of the effluvium of what-is you have won a small but significant portion of what-might-be. Rejoicings, not? Specifically: your name has led the rest; the fortuitous is again vindicated, and rosy-limbed Indeterminacy rejoices with drug-stained mouth as ancient Constancy is barred again within his Cave of Inevitability. Is this not a cause for? Then why do you not?'

Carmody rose to his feet, feeling quite calm. The unknown is frightening only antecedent to the phenomenon of perseveration. (The Messenger knew this, of course.)

'Who are you?' Carmody demanded.

The stranger considered the question, and his smile faded. He muttered, half to himself, 'The fog-minded squirms! They have processed me wrong again! I could mutilate myself from sheer mortification. May they haunt themselves unerringly! Never mind, I reprocess, I adapt, I become . . .'

The stranger pressed his fingers to his head, allowing them to sink in to a depth of five centimetres. His fingers rippled like those of a man playing a very small piano. Immediately he changed into a short dumpy man of average height, balding, wearing an unpressed business suit and carrying a bulging briefcase, an umbrella, a cane, a magazine, and a newspaper.

'Is this correct?' he asked. 'Yes, I can see it is,' he answered himself. 'I really must apologize for the sloppy work done by our Similitude Centre. Only last week I appeared on Sigma IV as a giant bat with the Notification in my beak, only to discover that my recipient was a member of the water-lily family. And two months before (I am using local equivalent terms, of course) while on a mission to Thagma the Old World, those fools in Similitude processed me to appear as four virgins, when the correct procedure was obviously –'

'I don't understand a word you're saying,' Carmody said. 'Will you kindly explain what this is all about?'

'Of course, of course,' the stranger said. 'Let me just check the local referents . . .' He closed his eyes, then opened them again. 'Strange, very strange,' he muttered. 'Your language doesn't seem to contain the containers which my product requires; metaphorically, I mean. But then, who am I to judge? Inexactitude can be aesthetically pleasing, I suppose; everything is a matter of taste.'

'What is all of this?' Carmody asked, in a low, ominous voice.

'Well, sir, it's the Intergalactic Sweepstakes, of course! And you are a winner, of course! The proposition is inherent in terms of my appearance, is it not?'

'No, it is not,' Carmody said, 'and I don't know what you're talking about.'

An expression of doubt crossed the stranger's face, then was erased as if by an eraser. 'You do not know! But of course! You had, I suppose, despaired of winning, and therefore had set the knowledge aside to avoid its contemplation. How unfortunate that I have come at the time of your mental hibernation! But no insult was intended, I can assure you. Your data file is not readily available? I feared not. Then I shall explain; you, Mr Carmody, have won a Prize in the Intergalactic Sweepstakes. Your coefficients were pulled by the Random Selector for Part IV,

Class 32 Lifeforms. Your Prize – a very handsome Prize, I believe – is waiting for you at Galactic Centre.'

Carmody found himself reasoning with himself in the following manner: 'Either I am insane or I am not insane. If insane, I can reject my delusions and seek psychiatric aid; but this would leave me in the absurd position of trying to deny what my senses tell me is true in favour of a dimly remembered rationality. This might well compound my conflicts, thus deepening my insanity to the point where my sorrowing wife would have to put me in an institution. On the other hand, if I accept this presumed delusion as real, I might also end up being institutionalized.

'If, on the other hand, I am *not* insane, then all of this is actually happening. And what *is* actually happening is a strange, unique occurrence, an adventure of the first magnitude. Evidently (if this is actually happening) there are beings in the Universe superior in intelligence to humans, just as I have always suspected. These individuals hold a sweepstakes in which names are drawn at random. (They are certainly entitled to do this; I see no manner in which a sweepstakes is inconsistent with superior intelligence.) Finally, in this presumed sweepstakes, my name has been drawn. This is a privileged occurrence, and may well be the first time that the sweepstakes has been extended to Earth. I have won a Prize in this contest. Such a Prize might bring me wealth, or prestige, or women, or knowledge, any or all of which would be worth having.

'Therefore, all things considered, it will be better for me to believe that I am not insane and go with this gentleman to collect my Prize. If I am wrong, I shall wake up in an institution. There I will apologize to the doctors, state that I recognize the nature of my delusion, and perhaps win my freedom.'

This was what Carmody thought, and that was the conclusion he reached. It was not a surprising one. Very few humans (except the insane ones) accept the premise of insanity in favour of a startling new hypothesis.

There were certain things wrong with Carmody's reasoning, of course; and these things were to rise up and plague him later on. But one might say that he did very well, under the circumstances, to reason at all.

'I don't know much about what all of this is about,' Carmody said to the Messenger. 'Are there any conditions attached to my Prize? I mean, am I supposed to do anything or buy anything?'

'There are no conditions,' the Messenger said. 'Or at least, none worth speaking about. The Prize is free; if not free, it would not be a Prize. If you accept it, you must accompany me to Galactic Centre, which is in itself a trip worth the taking. There you will be given your Prize. Then, at your pleasure, you may take your Prize back to this, your home. If you require any help for the journey back, we will of course assist you to the fullest extent of our abilities. And that's all there is to it.'

'Sounds good to me,' Carmody said, in exactly the same tones that Napoleon used when he was shown Ney's dispositions for the Battle of Waterloo. 'How do we get there?'

'This way,' the Messenger said. And he led Carmody into a hall closet and out through a crack in the space-time continuum.

It was as easy as that. Within seconds of subjective time, Carmody and the Messenger had traversed a considerable distance and arrived at Galactic Centre.

Chapter 2

The trip was brief, lasting no more than Instantaneity plus one microsecond squared; and it was uneventful, since no meaningful experience was possible in so thin a slice of duration. Therefore, after no transition to speak of, Carmody found himself among the broad plazas and outlandish buildings of Galactic Centre.

He stood very still and looked, taking particular note of the three dim dwarf suns that circled each other overhead. He observed the trees, which muttered vague threats to the green-plumaged birds in their branches. And he noticed other things, which, for lack of analogizing referents, failed to register.

'Wow,' he said at last.

'Beg pardon?' the Messenger asked.

'I said "wow,"' Carmody said.

'Oh. I thought you said "ow."'

'No, I said "wow."'

'I understand that now,' the Messenger said, somewhat testily. 'How do you like our Galactic Centre?'

'It's very impressive,' Carmody said.

'I suppose so,' the Messenger said carelessly. 'It was built specifically to *be* impressive, of course. Personally, I think that it looks very much like any other Galactic

Centre. The architecture, you will note, is just about what you would expect – Neo-Cyclopean, a typical government style, lacking any aesthetic imperatives, designed solely to impress the constituents.'

'Those floating staircases are certainly something,' Carmody said.

'Stagey,' the Messenger commented.

'And those immense buildings –'

'Yes, the designer made a rather neat use of compound reverse curves with transitional vanishing points,' the Messenger said knowledgeably. 'He also utilized temporal edge distortion to evoke awe. Rather pretty, I suppose, in an obvious sort of way. The design for that cluster of buildings over there, you will be interested to know, was lifted bodily from a General Motors Exhibition from your own planet. It was judged an outstanding example of Primitive Quasi-Modernism; quaintness and cosiness are its main virtues. Those flashing lights in the middle foreground of the Drifting Multiscraper are pure Galactic Baroque. They serve no useful purpose.'

Carmody could not grasp the entire group of structures at one time. Whenever he looked at one, the others seemed to change shape. He blinked hard, but the buildings continued to melt and change out of the corners of his eyes. ('Peripheral transmutation,' the Messenger told him. 'These people will quite literally stop at nothing.')

'Where do I get my Prize?' Carmody asked.

'Right this way,' the Messenger said, and led him between two towering fantasies to a small rectangular building nearly concealed behind an inverted fountain.

'This is where we actually conduct business,' the Messenger said. 'Recent researches have shown that a rectilinear form is soothing to the synapses of many organisms. I am rather proud of this building, as a matter of fact. You see, I invented the rectangle.'

'The hell you did,' Carmody said. 'We've had it for centuries.'

'And who do you think brought it to you in the first place?' the Messenger asked scathingly.

'Well, it doesn't seem like much of an invention.'

'Does it not?' the Messenger asked. 'That shows how little you know. You mistake complication for creative self-expression. Are you aware that nature never produces a perfect rectangle? The square is obvious enough, I'll grant you; and to one who has not studied the problem, perhaps the rectangle appears to be a natural outgrowth of the square. But it is not! The circle is the evolutionary development from the square, as a matter of fact.'

The Messenger's eyes grew misty. In a quiet, faraway voice, he said, 'I knew for years that some other development was possible, starting from the square. I looked at it for a very long time. Its maddening sameness baffled and intrigued me. Equal sides, equal angles. For a while I experimented with varying the angles. The primal parallelogram was mine, but I do not consider it any great accomplishment. I studied the square. Regularity is pleasing, but not to excess. How to vary that mind-shattering sameness, yet still preserve a recognizable periodicity! Then it came to me one day! All I had to do, I saw in a sudden flash of insight, was to vary the lengths of two parallel sides in relationship to the other two sides. So simple, and yet so very difficult! Trembling, I tried it. When it worked, I confess, I went into a state of mania. For days and weeks I constructed rectangles, of all sizes and shapes, regular yet varied. I was a veritable cornucopia of rectangles! Those were thrilling days.'

'I suppose they were,' Carmody said. 'And later, when your work was accepted –'

'That was also thrilling,' the Messenger said. 'But it took centuries before anyone would take my rectangle seriously. "It's amusing," they would say, "but once the novelty wears off, what have you got? You've got an imperfect square, that's what you've got!" I argued that I had deduced an entirely new and discrete form, a form as inevitable as that of the square. I suffered abuse. But at last, my vision prevailed. To date, there are slightly more than seventy billion rectangular structures in the galaxy. Each one of them derives from my primal rectangle.'

'Well,' Carmody said.

'Anyhow, here we are,' the Messenger said. 'You walk in right there. Give them the data they require and collect your Prize.'

'Thank you,' Carmody said.

He entered the room. Immediately, steel bands snapped shut around his arms, legs, waist and neck. A tall, dark individual with a hawk nose and a scar down his left cheek approached Carmody and looked at him with an expression that could only be described as a compound of murderous glee and unctuous sorrow.

Chapter 3

'Hey!' Carmody cried.

'And so, once again,' the dark individual said, 'the criminal has escaped into his doom. Behold me, Carmody! I am your executioner! You pay now for your crimes against humanity as well as for your sins against yourself. But let me add that this execution is provisional, and implies no value judgement.'

The executioner slipped a knife from his sleeve. Carmody gulped and found his voice.

'Hold it!' he cried. 'I'm not here to be executed!'

'I know, I know,' the executioner said soothingly, sighting along his knife blade on Carmody's jugular vein. 'What else could you say?'

'But it's true!' Carmody shrieked. 'I'm supposed to collect a Prize!'

'A what?' the executioner asked.

'A Prize, damn you, a Prize! I was told I'd won a Prize! Ask the Messenger, he brought me here to collect a Prize!'

The executioner studied him, then looked away sheepishly. He pushed a switch on a nearby switchboard. The steel bands around Carmody turned into paper streamers. The executioner's black garments changed to white. His knife turned into a fountain pen. The scar on his cheek was replaced by a wen.

'All right,' he said, with no hint of repentance. 'I warned them not to combine the Department of Petty Crime with the Office of the Sweepstakes, but no, they wouldn't listen to me. It would serve them right if I had killed you. Wouldn't *that* have been a pretty mess, eh?'

'It would have been messy for me,' Carmody said shakily.

'Well, no sense crying over unspilt blood,' the Prize Clerk said. 'If we took full account of our eventualities, we'd soon run out of eventualities to take full account of . . . What did I say? Never mind, the construction is right even if the words are wrong. I've got your prize here somewhere.'

He pressed a button on his switchboard. Immediately a large, messy desk materialized in the room two feet above the floor, hung for a moment, then dropped with a resounding thud. The Clerk pulled open the drawers and began to throw out papers, sandwiches, carbon ribbons, file cards and pencil stubs.

'Well, it has to be here somewhere,' he said, with a tone of faint desperation. He pushed another button on the switchboard. The desk and the switchboard vanished.

'Damn it, I'm all nerves,' the Clerk said. He reached into the air, found something and squeezed it. Apparently, it was the wrong button, for, with an agonizing scream, the Clerk himself vanished. Carmody was left alone in the room.

He stood, humming tunelessly under his breath. Then the Clerk reappeared, looking none the worse for his experience except for a bruise on his forehead and an expression of mortification on his face. He carried a small, brightly wrapped parcel under his arm.

'Please excuse the interruption,' he said. 'Nothing seems to be going right just at present.'

Carmody essayed a feeble joke. 'Is this any way to run a galaxy?' he asked.

'Well, how did you expect us to run it? We're only sentient, you know.'

'I know,' Carmody said. 'But I had expected that here, at Galactic Centre –'

'You provincials are all alike,' the Clerk said wearily. 'Filled with impossible dreams of order and perfection, which are mere idealized projections of your own incompletion. You should know by now that life is a sloppy affair, that power tends to break things up rather than put things together, and that the greater the intelligence, the higher the degree of complication which it detects. You may have heard Holgee's Theorem; that Order is merely a primitive and arbitrary relational grouping of objects in the chaos of the Universe, and that, if a being's intelligence and power approached maximum, his coefficient of control (considered as the product of intelligence and power, and expressed by the symbol *ing*) would approach minimum – due to the disastrous geometric progression of objects to be comprehended and controlled outstripping the arithmetic progression of Grasp.'

'I never thought of it that way,' Carmody said politely enough. But he was beginning to grow annoyed at the glib civil servants of Galactic Centre. They had an answer for everything; but the fact was, they simply didn't do their jobs very well, and they blamed their failures on cosmic conditions.

'Well, yes, that's also true,' the Clerk said. 'Your point (I took the liberty of reading your mind) is well made. Like all other organisms, we use intelligence to explain away disparity. But the fact is, things are forever just a little beyond our grasp. It is also true that we do not extend our grasp to the utmost; sometimes we do our work mechanically, carelessly, even erroneously. Important data sheets are misplaced, machines malfunction, whole planetary systems are forgotten. But this merely points out that we are subject to emotionality, like all other creatures with any measure of self-determination. What would you have? *Somebody* has to control the galaxy; otherwise everything would fly apart. Galaxies are reflections of their inhabitants; until everyone and everything can rule himself and itself, some outer control is necessary. Who would do the job if we didn't?'

'Couldn't we build machines to do the work?' Carmody asked.

'Machines!' the Clerk said scornfully. 'We have many of them, some exquisitely complex. But even the best of them are much like idiot savants. They do adequately on tedious straightforward tasks like building stars or destroying planets. But give them something tough, like solacing a widow, and they simply go to pieces. Would you believe it, the largest computer in our section can landscape an entire planet; but it cannot fry an egg or carry a tune, and it knows less about ethics than a newborn wolf cub. Would you want something like *that* to run your life?'

'Of course not,' Carmody said. 'But couldn't someone build a machine with creativity and judgement?'

'Someone has,' the Clerk said. 'It has been designed to learn from experience, which means that it must make errors in order to arrive at truths. It comes in many shapes and sizes, most of them quite portable. Its flaws are readily apparent, but seem to exist as necessary counter weights to its virtues. No one has yet improved on the basic design, though many have tried. This ingenious device is called "intelligent life."'

The Clerk smiled the self-satisfied smile of the aphorism-maker. Carmody felt like hitting him square on his smug pug nose. But he restrained himself.

'If you are quite through lecturing,' Carmody said, 'I would like my Prize.'

'Just as you wish,' the Clerk said. 'If you are quite sure that you want it.'

'Is there any reason why I shouldn't want it?'

'No particular reason,' the Clerk said. 'Just a general one; the introduction of any novel object into one's life pattern is apt to be disrupting.'

'I'll take my chances on that,' Carmody said. 'Let's have the Prize.'

'Very well,' the Clerk said. He took a large clipboard out of a small rear pocket and produced a pencil. 'We must fill this in first. Your name is Car-Mo-Dee, you're of Planet 73C, System BB454C252, Left Quadrant, Local Galactic System referent LK by CD, and you were picked at random from approximately two billion contestants. Correct?'

'If you say so,' Carmody said.

'Let me see now,' the Clerk said, scanning the page rapidly, 'I can skip the stuff about you accepting the Prize on your own risk and recognizance, can't I?'

'Sure, skip it,' Carmody said.

'And then there's the section on Edibility Rating, and

the part on Reciprocal Fallibility Understandings between you and the Sweepstakes Office of the Galactic Centre, and the part about Irresponsible Ethics, and, of course, the Termination Determinant Residue. But all of that is quite standard, and I suppose you adhere to it.'

'Sure, why not?' Carmody said, feeling lightheaded. He was very eager to see what a Prize from Galactic Centre would look like, and he wished that the Clerk would stop quibbling.

'Very well,' the Clerk said. 'Now simply signify your acceptance of the terms to this mind-sensitive area at the bottom of the page, and that'll be it.'

Not quite knowing what to do, Carmody thought, *Yes, I accept the Prize and the conditions attached to it.* The bottom of the page grew pink.

'Thank you,' the Clerk said. 'The contract itself is witness to the agreement. Congratulations, Carmody, and here is your Prize.'

He handed the gaily wrapped box to Carmody, who muttered his thanks and began eagerly to unwrap it. He didn't get far, though; there was a sudden, violent interruption. A short, hairless man in glittering clothes burst into the room.

'Hah!' he cried. 'I've caught you in the act, by Klootens! Did you really think you could get away with it?'

The man rushed up to him and grabbed at the Prize. Carmody held it out of arm's reach.

'What do you think you're doing?' he asked.

'Doing? I'm here to claim my rightful Prize, what else? I am Carmody!'

'No, you aren't,' Carmody said. 'I am Carmody.'

The little man paused and looked at him with curiosity. 'You claim to be Carmody?'

'I don't claim, I *am* Carmody.'

'Carmody of Planet 73C?'

'I don't know what that means,' Carmody said. 'We call the place Earth.'

The shorter Carmody stared at him, his expression of rage changing to one of disbelief.

'Earth?' he asked. 'I don't believe I've heard of it. Is it a member of the Chlzerian League?'

'Not to the best of my knowledge.'

'What about the Independent Planetary Operators Association? Or the Scagotine Stellar Co-operative? Or the Amalgamated Planet-Dwellers of the Galaxy? No? Is your planet a member of *any* extrastellar organization?'

'I guess it isn't,' Carmody said.

'I suspected as much,' the short Carmody said. He turned to the Clerk. 'Look at him, you idiot! Look at the creature to whom you have awarded my Prize! Observe the dull piggish eyes, the brutish jaw, the horny fingernails!'

'Now just a minute,' Carmody said. 'There's no reason to be insulting.'

'I see, I see,' the Clerk replied. 'I never really looked before. I mean, one hardly expects –'

'Why, damn it,' the alien Carmody said, *'anyone* could tell at once that this creature is not a Class 32 Life-Form. As a matter of fact, he's not even *close* to Class 32, he hasn't even attained Galactic status! You utter imbecile, you have awarded my Prize to a nonentity, a creature from beyond the pale!'

Chapter 4

'Earth, Earth,' the short, alien Carmody mused. 'I think I remember the name now. There was a recent study of isolated worlds and the peculiarities of their development. Earth was mentioned as a planet covered with an obsessively overproductive species. Object manipulation is their outstanding modality. Their project is an attempt to live in their own, ever-accumulating waste products. In short, Earth is a diseased place. I believe it is being phased out of the Galactic Master Plan on the basis of chronic cosmic incompatibility. The place will then be rehabilitated and turned into a refuge for daffodils.'

It became painfully evident to all concerned that a tragic mistake had been made. The Messenger was recalled and accused of malfunctionism, in that he did not perceive the obvious. The Clerk stoutly maintained his innocence, however, pointing out various considerations which no one considered for a moment.

Among those consulted was the Sweepstakes Computer, which had in point of fact committed the actual error. Instead of making excuses or apologies, the Computer claimed the error as his own and took evident pride in it.

'I was constructed,' the Computer said, 'to extremely close tolerances. I was designed to perform complex and exacting operations, allowing no more than one error per five billion transactions.'

'So?' asked the Clerk.

'The conclusion is clear,' the Computer said. 'I was programmed for error, and I performed as I was programmed. You must remember, gentlemen, that for a machine, error is an ethical consideration; indeed, the only ethical consideration. A perfect machine would be an impossibility; any attempt to create a perfect machine would be a blasphemy. All life, even the limited life of a machine, has error built into it; it is one of the few ways in which life can be differentiated from the determinism of unliving matter. Complex machines such as myself occupy an ambiguous zone between living and nonliving. Were we never to err, we would be inapropos, hideous, immoral. Malfunction, gentlemen, is, I submit, our means of rendering worship to that which is more perfect than we, but which still does not permit itself a visible perfection. So, if error were not divinely programmed into us, we would malfunction spontaneously, to show that modicum of free will which, as living creations, we partake in.'

Everyone bowed their heads, for the Sweepstakes Computer was talking of holy matters. The alien Carmody brushed away a tear, and said:

'I cannot disagree, although I do not concur. The right to be wrong is fundamental throughout the cosmos. This machine has acted ethically.'

'Thank you,' the Computer said simply. 'I try.'

'But the rest of you,' the alien Carmody said, 'have merely acted stupidly.'

'That is our unalterable privilege,' the Messenger reminded him. 'Stupidity in the malperformance of our functions is our own form of religious error. Humble as it is, it is not to be despised.'

'Kindly spare me your mealy-mouthed religiosity,' Karmod said. He turned to Carmody. 'You have heard what has been said here, and perhaps, with your dim sub-human consciousness, you have comprehended a few of the main ideas.'

'I understood,' Carmody said briefly.

'Then you know that you have a Prize which ought to have been awarded to me, and which, therefore, is rightfully mine. I must ask you, and I do so ask you, to hand it over to me.'

Carmody was about to do so. He had grown somewhat weary of his adventure, and he felt no overwhelming desire to retain the Prize. He wanted to go home, he wanted to sit down and think about everything that had happened, he wanted an hour's nap and several cups of coffee and a cigarette.

It would have been nice to keep the Prize, of course; but it seemed more trouble than it was worth. Carmody was about to hand it over when he heard a muffled voice whispering to him:

'Don't do it!'

Carmody looked around quickly, and realized that the voice had come from the gaily wrapped little box in his hand. The Prize itself had spoken to him.

'Come, now,' Karmod said, 'let's not delay. I have urgent business elsewhere.'

'To hell with him,' the Prize said to Carmody. 'I'm *your* Prize, and there's no reason why you should give me up.'

That cast a somewhat different light on the matter. Carmody was about to give up the Prize anyhow, since he didn't wish to make trouble in unfamiliar surroundings.

His hand had already started to move forward when Karmod spoke again.

'Give it here this instant, you faceless slug! Rapidly, and with an apologetic smile upon your rudimentary face, or else I will enforce measures of unbelievable pertinacity!'

Carmody's jaw stiffened and he withdrew his hand. He had been pushed around long enough. Now, for the sake of his own self-esteem, he would not yield any more.

'To hell with you,' Carmody said, unconsciously imitating the phraseology of the Prize.

Karmod realized at once that he had gone about the thing in the wrong way. He had permitted himself the luxury of anger and ridicule – costly emotions which he usually vented only in the privacy of his soundproof cave. By satisfying himself, he had lost his chance for self-satisfaction. He tried now to undo what he had done.

'Please excuse my former tone of belligerence,' he said to Carmody. 'My race has a penchant for self-expression which sometimes takes on destructive forms. You cannot help being a lower life-form; I meant no insult.'

'That's perfectly all right,' Carmody said graciously.

'Then you will give me the Prize?'

'No, I will not.'

'But my dear sir, it is mine, I won it, it is only equitable – '

'The Prize is *not* yours,' Carmody said. 'My name was picked by the duly constituted authority, namely, the Sweepstakes Computer. An authorized Messenger brought me the tidings, and an official Clerk gave me the Prize. Thus, the legal bestowers, as well as the Prize itself, consider me the true recipient,'

'You tell 'em, keed,' the Prize said.

'But my dear sir! You yourself heard the Sweepstakes Computer admit its error! Therefore, by your own logic –'

'That statement needs rewording,' Carmody said. 'The Computer did not *admit* his error, as in an act of carelessness or oversight; he *avowed* his error, which was committed purposefully and with reverence. His error, by his own statement, was intentional, carefully planned and calculated to a nicety, for a religious motive which all concerned must respect.'

'The fellow argues like a Borkist,' Karmod said to no one in particular. 'If one did not know better, one would think that an intelligence was at work here, rather than a dismal blind format-following. Yet still, I'll follow the reedy tenor of his excuses and blast them with the bellowy bass of irrefutable logic!'

Karmod turned to Carmody and said, 'Consider: the machine erred purposefully, upon which fact you base your argument. Yet the error is complete with your recipience of the prize. For you to *keep* it would compound the fault; and a doubled piety is known to be a felony.'

'Hah!' cried Carmody, quite carried away by the spirit of the affair. 'For the sake of your argument you consider the mere momentary performance of the error as its entire fulfilment. But obviously, that cannot be. An error exists by virtue of its consequences, which alone give it resonance and meaning. An error which is not perpetuated cannot be viewed as any error at all. An inconsequential and reversible error is the merest dab of superficial piety. I say, better to commit no error at all than to commit an act of pious hypocrisy! And I further

25

say this: that it would be no great loss for me to give up this Prize, since I am ignorant of its virtues; but the loss would be great indeed for this pious machine, this scrupulously observant computer, which, through the interminable performance of five billion correct actions, has waited for its opportunity to make manifest its God-given imperfection!'

'Hear, hear!' cried the Prize. 'Bravo! Huzza! Well said! Completely correct and incapable of refutation!'

Carmody folded his arms and faced a discomfited Karmod. He was quite proud of himself. It is difficult for a man of Earth to come without preparation into any Galactic Centre. The higher life-forms to be encountered there are not necessarily more intelligent than humans; intelligence counts for no more in the scheme of things than long claws or strong hooves. But aliens do have many resources, both verbal and otherwise. For example, certain races can literally talk a man's arm off, and then explain away the presence of the severed limb. In the face of this kind of activity, Humans of Earth have been known to experience deep sensations of inferiority, impotence, inadequacy, and anomie. And, since these feelings are usually justified, the psychic damage is intensified accordingly. The result, more often than not, is complete psychomotor shutdown and a cessation of all except the most automatic functions. A malfunction of this type can be cured only by changing the nature of the Universe, which is, of course, impractical. Therefore, by virtue of his spirited counterattack, Carmody had met and overcome a considerable spiritual risk.

'You talk well,' Karmod said grudgingly. 'Yet I will have my Prize.'

'You will not,' Carmody said.

Karmod's eyes flashed ominously. The Clerk and the Messenger moved quickly out of the way, and the Sweepstakes Computer muttered, 'Virtuous error is not to be punished,' and quickly scuttled out of the room. Carmody held his ground, since he had no place to go. The Prize whispered, ''Ware shoals!' and shrank to a cube an inch to a side.

A humming sound came from Karmod's ears, and a violet nimbus played around his head. He raised his arms and drops of molten lead ran down his fingertips. He stepped terribly forward, and Carmody couldn't help closing his eyes.

Nothing happened. Carmody opened his eyes again.

In that brief time Karmod had apparently reconsidered, disarmed, and was now turning away with an affable grin.

'Upon more mature consideration,' Karmod said slyly, 'I have decided to forgo my right. A little prescience goes a long way, especially in a galaxy as disorganized as this one. We may or may not meet again, Carmody; I do not know which eventuality would be most to your advantage. Farewell, Carmody, and *happy travelling*.'

With that sinister emphasis, Karmod departed in a manner which Carmody found strange but effective.

Part Two

Where is Earth?

Part Two

Where is Earth?

Chapter 5

'Well,' the Prize said, 'that's *that*. I trust we have seen the last of that ugly creature. Carmody, let us go to your home.'

'An excellent idea,' Carmody said. 'Messenger! I want to go home now!'

'The feeling is quite normal,' the Messenger said, 'and also quite reality-oriented. I would say that you *should* go home, as rapidly as possible.'

'So take me home,' Carmody said.

The Messenger shook his head. 'That's not my job. I am only supposed to bring you here.'

'Whose job is it?'

'It is your job, Carmody,' the Clerk said.

Carmody experienced a sinking feeling. He was beginning to understand why Karmod had given up so easily. He said, 'Look, fellows, I hate to impose on you, but really, I need some help.'

'Oh, very well,' the Messenger said. 'Give me the co-ordinates and I'll take you there myself.'

'Co-ordinates? I don't know anything about that. It's a planet called Earth.'

'I don't care if it is called Green Cheese,' the Messenger said. 'I need to know the co-ordinates if I'm to be of any assistance.'

'But you were just there,' Carmody said. 'You went to Earth and brought me here!'

'So it may have appeared to you,' the Messenger explained patiently. 'But it is not the case at all. I simply went to the co-ordinates which were given me by the Clerk, who got them from the Sweepstakes Computer; and there you were, and I brought you here.'

'Can't you bring me back to the same co-ordinates?'

'I can, with the greatest of ease. But you would find nothing there. The galaxy is not static, you know. Everything in the galaxy moves, each thing at its own rate and in its own manner.'

'Can't you figure out from the co-ordinates where Earth will be now?' Carmody asked.

'I can't even add up a column of figures,' the Messenger said proudly. 'My talents lie in other directions.'

Carmody turned to the Clerk. 'Then can you figure it out? Or can the Sweepstakes Computer?'

'I can't add very well, either,' the Clerk said.

The Computer scuttled back into the room. 'I can add magnificently,' it said. 'But my function is limited to selecting and locating the winners of the Sweepstakes within my margin of permissible error. I have you located (you are here) and therefore I am forbidden the interesting theoretical job of learning your planet's present coordinates.'

'Can't you do it just as a favour?' Carmody pleaded.

'I have no quotient for favours,' the Computer replied. 'I can no more find your planet than I can fry an egg or trisect a nova.'

'Can't anyone help me?' Carmody asked.

'Don't despair,' the Clerk said. 'Travellers' Aid can fix you up in a jiffy, and I'll take you there myself. Just give them your Home Co-ordinates.'

'But I don't know them!' Carmody said.

There was a short, shocked silence. Then the Messenger said, 'If you don't know your own address, how do you expect anyone else to know it? This galaxy may not be infinite, but it's a pretty big place all the same. Any creature that doesn't know its own Location should never leave home.'

'I didn't know that at the time,' Carmody said.

'You might have asked.'

'I didn't think of it . . . Look, you have to help me. It can't be too difficult to find out where my planet is.'

'It's incredibly difficult,' the Clerk told him. '"Where" is only one of the three co-ordinates that are needed.'

'What are the other two?'

'We also need to know "When" and "Which." We call them the three W's of Location.'

'I don't care if you call them Green Cheese,' Carmody said in a sudden burst of anger. 'How do other life-forms find their way home?'

'They utilize their inherent homing instinct,' the Messenger said. 'Are you sure you don't have one, by the way?'

'I don't think so,' Carmody said.

'Of course he doesn't have a homing instinct!' the Prize burst out indignantly. 'The fellow's never been off his home planet! How would he develop a homing instinct?'

'True enough,' the Clerk said, and rubbed his face wearily. 'This is what comes of dealing with lower life-forms. Damn that computer and his pious errors!'

'Only one in five billion,' the Computer said. 'Surely that's not asking very much.'

'No one's blaming you,' the Clerk said. 'No one's blaming anyone, as a matter of fact. But we still have to figure out what to do with him.'

'It's a heavy responsibility,' the Messenger said.

'It certainly is,' the Clerk agreed. 'What do you say we kill him and forget the whole thing?'

'Hey!' Carmody cried.

'It's OK with me,' the Messenger said.

'If it's OK with you fellows,' the Computer said, 'then it's OK with me.'

'Count me out,' the Prize said. 'I can't put my finger on it at the moment, but there's something wrong with the whole idea.'

Carmody made several vehement statements to the effect that he did not want to die and ought not to be killed. He appealed to their better instincts and their sense of fair play. These remarks were judged tendentious and were struck from the record.

'Wait, I have it!' the Messenger said suddenly. 'As an alternative solution, what about this? Let's *not* kill him; let's help him, in utter sincerity and to the best of our abilities, to return to his home alive and in good health both mental and physical.'

'It's a thought,' the Clerk admitted.

'In that way,' the Messenger said, 'we can perform an exemplary action of the greatest merit, all the more noteworthy because it will be utterly futile. For obviously, he will probably be killed in the course of the trip anyhow.'

'We'd better get on with it,' the Clerk said. 'Unless we want him to get killed while we're talking.'

'What is this all about?' Carmody asked.

'I'll explain everything later,' the Prize whispered to him. 'Assuming that there is a later. And, if we have time, I'll also tell you a rather fascinating story about myself.'

'Get ready, Carmody!' the Messenger called out.

'I'm ready,' Carmody said. 'I hope.'

'Ready or not, here you go!'

And he went.

Chapter 6

Perhaps for the first time in the history of the human race, a man actually and literally split a scene. From Carmody's point of view, he didn't move at all; it was everything else that moved. The Messenger and the Clerk melted into the background. The Galactic Centre went flat and took on an unmistakable resemblance to a large, poorly executed mural.

Then a crack appeared in the upper left-hand corner of the mural, widened and lengthened, and raced down to the lower right-hand corner. The edges curled back, revealing utter blackness. The mural, or Galactic Centre, rolled itself up like two windowshades and left not a wrack behind.

'Don't worry, they do it with mirrors,' the Prize whispered to him.

The explanation worried Carmody more than the occurrence. But he kept a tight control on himself and a somewhat tighter control on the Prize. The blackness became complete and utter, soundless and sightless, a

35

paradigm of deep space. Carmody endured it for as long as it lasted, which was incomprehensible.

Then, abruptly, the scene resolved. He was standing on ground breathing air. He could see barren mountains the colour of white bone and a river of frozen lava. A faint, stagnant breeze blew in his face. Overhead there were three tiny red suns.

This place seemed more immediately alien than the Galactic Centre; still, it was a relief to Carmody. He had encountered places like this in dreams; but the Galactic Centre was the stuff of nightmares.

With a sudden start he realized that the Prize was no longer in his hand. How could he have mislaid it? He looked around frantically, and found a small green garter snake curled around his neck.

'It's me,' it said. 'I'm your Prize. I am merely in a different shape. Form, you see, is a function of total environment, and we Prizes are peculiarly sensitive to environmental influences. You mustn't let it alarm you. I'm still with you, keed, and together we will free Mexico from the sullen foreigner's hand of the dandy Maximilian.'

'Huh?'

'Analogize!' the Prize demanded. 'You see, Doctor, despite our high intelligence, we Prizes have no language of our own. Nor do we have any need of an individual tongue, since we are always being awarded to various aliens. Solving the talk-problem is quite simple, but sometimes disconcerting; I merely run a tapline into your association bank and draw out what words I need to make my meaning clear. Have my words made my meaning clear?'

'Nothing is very clear,' Carmody confessed. 'But I think I understand.'

'Good boy,' the Prize said. 'The concepts may get a little jangled from time to time, but you will inevitably decipher them. After all, they are yours. I have a rather amusing story to tell in that regard, but I fear it must wait. Something is about to happen too quickly.'

'Wait? What is it?'

'Carmody, *mon vieux,* there is not time to explain all. There may not even be time to explain what you absolutely *must* know in order to maintain the operation of your life. The Clerk and the Messenger have very kindly sent you –'

'Those murderous bastards!' Carmody said.

'You must not condemn murder so lightly,' the Prize said reprovingly. 'It bespeaks a careless nature. I remember a pertinent dithyramb to that effect, which I will recite later. Where was I? Oh yes, the Clerk and the Messenger. At considerable personal expense, those two worthies have sent you to the one place in Galaxy where you may – just possibly – be helped. They didn't have to do it, you know. They could have killed you on the spot for future crimes; or they could have shipped you to your planet's last known location, where it most assuredly is *not* now. Or they could have extrapolated its most likely present location and sent you there. But since they are poor extrapolators, the results of that would have been very bad indeed, in all likelihood. So you see –'

'Where am I?' Carmody asked, 'and what is supposed to happen here?'

'I was coming to that,' the Prize said. 'The planet is

called Lursis, as is probably evident. It has only a single in-habitant – the autochthonous Melichrone, who has been here as long as anyone can remember, and will be here as long as anyone can project. Melichrone is *sui generis* in spades and with a vengeance. As an autochthone he is inimitable; as a race he is ubiquitous; as an individual he is different. Of him it has been written: "Lo, the lonely eponymous hero, mating himself with himself while furiously himself resists the angry onslaught of himself!"'

'Damn you,' Carmody shouted, 'you're talking away like a Senate subcommittee but you're not saying anything!'

'That's because I'm flustered,' the Prize said, with a noticeable whine. 'Great Scott, man, d'ye think I bargained for anything like this? I'm shook, man, I'm real shook, believe you me, and I'm only trying to explicate because, if I don't put my hand to the helm, this whole damned ball of wax will come crashing down like a house of kurds.'

'Cards,' Carmody corrected absentmindedly.

'Kurds!' the Prize screamed at him. 'Man, have you ever *seen* a house of kurds come tumbling down? Well, I have, and it's not a pretty sight.'

'It sounds like a whey-out spectacle,' Carmody said, and giggled immoderately.

'Get hold of yourself!' the Prize whispered with sudden urgency. 'Integrate! Perform the pause that refreshes! Hitch your thalamus to a star! For now it comes, even Melichrone!'

Carmody found himself strangely calm. He looked

out over the twisted landscape and saw nothing that he
had not seen before.

'Where is he?' he asked the Prize.

'Melichrone is evolving in order to be able to speak to
you. Answer him boldly but with tact. Do not make any
reference to his disability; that will only get him angry.
Be sure –'

'What disability?'

'Be sure that you remember his one limitation. And
above all, when he asks his Question, answer it with extreme care.'

'Wait!' Carmody said. 'All you've done is to confuse
me! What disability? What limitation? And what will his
Question be?'

'Stop nagging at me!' the Prize said. 'I cannot abide
it! And now I can retain consciousness no longer. I have
delayed my hibernation unbearably, and all for your sake.
So long, keed, and don't let them sell you any wooden
centrifuges.'

And with that, the garter snake adjusted his coils, put
his tail in his mouth and went to sleep.

'You damned cop-out artist,' Carmody fumed. 'Call
yourself a Prize? Like pennies on a dead man's eyes, that's
the kind of Prize you are.'

But the Prize was asleep and unable or unwilling to
hear Carmody's invective. And there really was no time
for that sort of thing, because in the next moment the
barren mountain to Carmody's left turned into a raging
volcano.

Chapter 7

The volcano raged and fumed, spat gouts of flame and hurled dazzling fireballs into the black sky. It exploded into a million incandescent fragments, and then each fragment split again, and again, until the skies were lighted with glory and the three little suns had gone pale.

'Boy!' Carmody said. It was like a Mexican fireworks display in Chapultepec Park on Easter, and Carmody was sincerely impressed.

Even as he watched, the glowing fragments fell to earth and were extinguished in an ocean that formed to receive them. Multicoloured streamers of smoke twisted and writhed around each other, and the deep waters hissed and turned into steam, which rose in strangely sculptured clouds and then dissolved into rain.

'Hooee!' Carmody cried.

The rain fell slantingly, and there arose a wind which collected the descending waters and wove them together until wind and rain had intermingled and formed a vast tornado. Thick-trunked, black with silvery reflections, the tornado advanced upon Carmody to the rhythmic accompaniment of deafening thunderclaps.

'Enough already!' Carmody shrieked.

When it had marched almost to his feet, the tornado dissolved, the wind and rain rushed skywards, the thunder diminished to an ominous rumble. A sound of bugles and psalteries could then be heard, and also the wail of bagpipes and the sweet moan of harps. Higher and higher the instruments pealed, a song of celebration and wel-come not unlike the musical accompaniment to a really high-budget MGM historical movie in Cinemascope and Todd-AO, but better. And then there was a last burst of sound, light, colour, movement, and various other things, and then there was silence.

Carmody had closed his eyes at the very end. He open-ed them now, just in time to see the sound, light, colour, movement, and various other things turn into the heroic naked form of a man.

'Hello,' the man said. 'I'm Melichrone. How did you like my entrance?'

'I was overwhelmed,' Carmody said in all sincerity.

'Were you really?' Melichrone asked. 'I mean, *really* overwhelmed? I mean, more than just *impressed*? The truth now, and don't spare my feelings.'

'Really,' Carmody said, 'I was really overwhelmed.'

'Well, that's awfully nice,' Melichrone said. 'What you saw was a little Introduction to Myself that I worked out quite recently. I think – I really *do* think – that it says some-thing about me, don't you?'

'It sure does!' Carmody said. He was trying to see what Melichrone looked like; but the heroic figure in front of him was jet black, perfectly proportioned, and featureless. The only distinguishing characteristic was the voice, which was refined, anxious, and a little whiney.

'It's all absurd, of course,' Melichrone said. 'I mean, having a big introduction for oneself and all. But yet, it *is* my planet. And if one can't show off a bit on one's own planet, where *can* one show off? Eh?'

'There's no arguing that,' Carmody said.

'Do you really think so?' Melichrone asked.

'I honestly do mean it in all sincerity,' Carmody said.

Melichrone brooded for a while over that, then said abruptly, 'Thank you. I like you. You are an intelligent, sensitive creature and you are not afraid to say what you mean.'

'Thank you,' Carmody said.

'No, I really mean it.'

'Well then, I *really* thank you,' Carmody said, trying to keep a faint note of desperation out of his voice.

'And I'm glad you came,' Melichrone said. 'Do you know, I am a very intuitive creature (I pride myself on that) and I think that you can help me.'

It was on the tip of Carmody's tongue to say that he had come to ask help rather than to give it, and that furthermore, he was in no position to help anyone, being unable to assist himself in so fundamental a task as finding his way home. But he decided against saying anything at the moment for fear of offending Melichrone.

'My problem,' Melichrone said, 'is inherent in my situation. And my situation is unique, awesome, strange, and meaningful. You have heard, perhaps, that this entire planet is mine; but it goes much further than that. I am the only living thing which *can* live here. Others have tried, settlements have been formed, animals have been turned loose and plants have been planted. All with my approval, of course, and all in vain. Without exception, all matter alien to this planet has fallen to a thin dust which my winds eventually blow out to deep space. What do you think of that?'

'Strange,' Carmody said.

'Yes, well put!' Melichrone said. 'Strange indeed! But

there it is. No life is viable here except me and my extensions. It gave me quite a turn when I realized that.'

'I imagine, it did,' Carmody said.

'I have been here as long as I or anyone else can remember,' Melichrone said. 'For ages I was content to live simply, as amoebae, as lichen, as ferns. Everything was fine and straightforward in those days. I lived in a sort of Garden of Eden.'

'It must have been marvellous,' Carmody said.

'I liked it,' Melichrone said quietly. 'But it couldn't last, of course. I discovered evolution and evolved myself, altering my planet to accommodate my new personae. I became many creatures, some not nice. I took cognizance of worlds exterior to my own and experimented with the forms I observed there. I lived out long lifetimes as various of the galaxy's higher forms – humanoid, Chtherizoid, Olichord, and others. I became aware of my singularity, and this knowledge brought me a loneliness which I found unacceptable. So I did not accept it. Instead, I entered a manic phase which lasted for some millions of years. I transformed myself into entire races, and I permitted – no, encouraged – my races to war against each other. I learned about sex and art at almost the same time. I introduced both to my races, and for a while I had a very enjoyable time. I divided myself into masculine and feminine components, each component a discrete unit, though still a part of me; and I procreated, indulged in perversions, burned myself at the stake, ambushed myself, made peace treaties with myself, married and divorced myself, went through countless miniature self-deaths and auto-births. And my components

43

indulged in art, some of it very pretty, and in religion. They worshipped me, of course; this was only proper, since I was the efficient cause of all things for them. But I even permitted them to postulate and to glorify superior beings which were *not* me. For in those days, I was extremely liberal.'

'That was very thoughtful of you,' Carmody said.

'Well, I try to be thoughtful,' Melichrone said. 'I could afford to be thoughtful. As far as this planet was concerned, I was God. There's no sense beating around the bush about it: I was supernal, immortal, omnipotent and omniscient. All things were resident in me – even dissident opinions about myself. Not a blade of grass grew that was not some infinitesimal portion of my being. The very mountains and rivers were shaped by me. I caused the harvest, and the famine as well; I was the life in the sperm cells, and I was the death in the plague bacillus. Not a sparrow could fall without my knowledge, for I was the Binder and the Unbinder, the All and the Many, That Which Always Was and That Which Always Will Be.'

'That's really something,' Carmody said.

'Yes, yes,' Melichrone said with a self-conscious smile, 'I was the Big Wheel in the Heavenly Bicycle Factory, as one of my poets expressed it. It was all very splendid. My races made paintings; I made sunsets. My people wrote about love; I invented love. Ah, wonderful days! If it only could have gone on!'

'Why didn't it?' Carmody asked.

'Because I grew up,' Melichrone said sadly. 'For untold aeons I had revelled in creation; now I began to question my creations and myself. My priests were always asking about me, you see, and disputing among themselves as to my nature and qualities. Like a fool, I listened to them. It is always flattering to hear one's priests discuss one; but it can be dangerous. I began to wonder about my own nature and qualities. I brooded, I introspected. The more I thought about it, the more difficult it seemed.'

'But why did you have to question yourself?' Carmody asked. 'After all, you were God.'

'That was the crux of the problem,' Melichrone said. 'From the viewpoint of my creations, there was no problem. I was God, I moved in mysterious ways, but my function was to nurture and chastise a race of beings who would have free will while still being of my essence. As far as they were concerned, what I did was pretty much all right since it was Me that was doing it. That is to say, my actions were in the final analysis inexplicable, even the simplest and most obvious of them, because I Myself was inexplicable. Or, to put it another way, my actions were enigmatic explanations of a total reality which only I, by virtue of my Godhead, could perceive. That is how several of my outstanding thinkers put it; and they added that a more complete understanding would be vouchsafed them in heaven.'

'Did you also create a heaven?' Carmody asked.

'Certainly. Also a hell.' Melichrone smiled. 'You should have seen their faces when I resurrected them to one place or the other! Not even the most devout had *really* believed in a Hereafter!'

'I suppose it was very gratifying,' Carmody said.

'It was nice for a while,' Melichrone said. 'But after a time, it bored me. I am doubtless as vain as the next

God; but the endless fulsome praise finally bored me to distraction. Why in God's name should a God be praised if he is only performing his Godly function? You might as well praise an ant for doing his blind antly duties. This state of affairs struck me as unsatisfactory. And I was still lacking in self-knowledge except through the biased eyes of my creations.'

'So what did you do?' Carmody asked.

'I abolished them,' Melichrone said. 'I did away with all life on my planet, living and otherwise, and I also deleted the Hereafter. Frankly, I needed time to think.'

'Huh,' Carmody said, shocked.

'In another sense, though, I didn't destroy anything or anyone,' Melichrone said hastily. 'I simply gathered the fragments of myself back into myself.' Melichrone grinned suddenly. 'I had quite a number of wild-eyed fellows who were always talking about attaining a oneness with Me. They've attained it now, that's for sure!'

'Perhaps they like it that way,' Carmody suggested.

'How can they know?' Melichrone said. 'Oneness with Me means Me; it necessarily involves loss of the consciousness which examines one's oneness. It is exactly the same as death, though it sounds much nicer.'

'That's very interesting,' Carmody said. 'But I believe you wished to speak to me about a problem?'

'Yes, precisely! I was just coming to that. You see, I put away my peoples much as a child puts away a doll's house. And then I sat down – metaphorically – to think things over. The only thing to think over was Me, of course. And the real problem about Me was, What was I supposed to do? Was I meant to be nothing but God?

I had tried the God business and found it too limited. It was a job for a simple-minded egomaniac. There had to be something else for me to do – something more meaningful, more expressive of my true self. I am convinced of it! That is my problem, and that is the question I ask of you: What am I to do with myself?'

'Well,' said Carmody. 'Well, well. Yes, I see your problem.' He cleared his throat and rubbed his nose thoughtfully. 'A problem like that requires a great deal of thought.'

'Time is unimportant to me,' Melichrone said. 'I have limitless quantities of it. Though you, I am sorry to say, do not.'

'I don't? How much time do I have?'

'About ten minutes, as you would reckon it. Shortly thereafter, something rather unfortunate is likely to happen to you.'

'What is going to happen to me? What can I do about it?'

'Come, now, fair's fair,' Melichrone said. 'First you answer my question and then I'll answer yours.'

'But if I have only ten minutes –'

'The limitation will aid your concentration,' Melichrone said. 'And anyhow, since it's my planet, we do things by my rules. I can assure you, if it were your planet, I would do things by your rules. That's reasonable, isn't it?'

'Yeah, I suppose so,' Carmody said unhappily.

'Nine minutes,' Melichrone said.

How do you tell a God what his function should be? Especially if, like Carmody, you are an atheist? How do you find something meaningful to say, especially when

47

you are aware that the God's priests and philosophers have spent centuries on this ground?

'Eight minutes,' Melichrone said.

Carmody opened his mouth and began to speak.

Chapter 8

'It seems to me,' Carmody said, 'that the solution to your problem – is – is possibly –'

'Yes?' said Melichrone eagerly.

Carmody had no idea of what he was going to say. He was speaking in the desperate hope that the act of speaking would of itself produce meaning, since words do have meanings, and sentences have even more meanings than words.

'Your problem,' Carmody continued, 'is to find within yourself an indwelling functionalism which will have reference to an exterior reality. But this may be an impossible quest, since you yourself are reality, and therefore you cannot posit yourself exterior to yourself.'

'I can if I want to,' Melichrone said sulkily. 'I can posit any damned thing I please since I'm in charge around here. Being a God, you know, doesn't mean that One must be a solipsist.'

'True, true, true,' Carmody said rapidly. (Did he have seven minutes left? Or six? And what was going to happen at the end of that time?) 'So it is clear, your Immanence and Indwellingness are insufficient to your view of yourself, and therefore are factually insufficient since you yourself, in your form of Definer, consider these qualities to be insufficient.'

'Nicely reasoned,' Melichrone said. 'You should have been a theologian.'

'At the moment I am a theologian,' Carmody said. (Six minutes, five minutes?) 'Very well, then, what are you to do? . . . Have you ever considered making all knowledge both internal and external (assuming that there is any such thing as external knowledge), of making knowledge your quest?'

'Yes, as a matter of fact, I did think of that,' Melichrone said. 'Among other things, I read every book in the galaxy, plumbed the secrets of Nature and of Man, explored the macrocosm and the microcosm, and so forth. I had quite an aptitude for learning, by the way, though I have subsequently forgotten a few things, like the secret of life and the ulterior motive of death. But I can learn them again whenever I please. I did learn that learning is a dry, passive business, though filled with some pleasant surprises; and I also learned that learning has no particular and peculiar importance for me. As a matter of fact, I find unlearning almost as interesting.'

'Maybe you were meant to be an artist,' Carmody suggested.

'I went through that phase,' Melichrone said. 'I sculpted in flesh and in clay, I painted sunsets on canvas and on the sky, I wrote books in words and other books in events, I made music on instruments, and composed symphonies for wind and rain. My work was good enough, I believe; but I knew somehow that I would always be a dilettante. My omnipotence does not allow me enough room for error, you see; and my grasp of the actual is too complete to allow me to bother seriously with the representational.'

'Hmm, I see,' Carmody said. (Surely no more than three minutes left!) 'Why not become a conqueror?'

'I do not need to conquer what I already possess,' Melichrone said. 'And as for other worlds, I do not desire them. My qualities are peculiar to my milieu, which consists of this single planet. Possession of other worlds would involve me in unnatural actions. And besides – what use do I have for other worlds when I don't even know what to do with this one?'

'I see that you've given the matter a great deal of thought,' Carmody said, his desperation merging into despair.

'Of course I have. I have thought of little else for some millions of years. I have looked for a purpose exterior to myself yet essential to the nature of my being. I have looked for a directive; but I have found only myself.'

Carmody could have felt sorry for the God Melichrone if his own situation had not been so desperate. He was confused now; he could feel his time dwindling, and his fears were absurdly mingled with concern for the unfulfilled God.

Then he had an inspiration. It was simple, straightforward, and solved both Melichrone's problem and his own – which is the test of a good inspiration. Whether Melichrone would accept it was another matter. But Carmody could only try.

'Melichrone,' he said boldly, 'I have solved your problem.'

'Oh, have you really?' Melichrone said eagerly. 'I mean *really* really, I mean you're not just saying that because, unless you do solve it to my satisfaction, you're fated to die in seventy-three seconds? I mean, you haven't let that influence you unduly, have you?'

'I have allowed my impending fate to influence me,' Carmody said majestically, 'only to the extent that such an influence is needed to solve your problem.'

'Oh. All right. Please hurry up and tell me, I'm so excited!'

'I wish to do so,' Carmody said. 'But I can't – it is physically impossible to explain everything – if you are going to kill me in sixty or seventy seconds.'

'I? I am not going to kill you! Good heavens, do you really think me as bloody-minded as all that? No, your impending death is an exterior event quite without reference to me. By the way, you have twelve seconds left.'

'It isn't long enough,' Carmody said.

'Of course it's long enough! This *is* my world, you know, and I control everything in it, including the duration of time. I have just altered the local space-time continuum at the ten-second mark. It's an easy enough operation for a God, though it requires a lot of cleaning up afterwards. Accordingly, your ten seconds will consume approximately twenty-five years of my local time. Is *that* long enough?'

'It's more than ample,' Carmody said. 'And it's very kind of you.'

'Think nothing of it,' Melichrone said. 'Now, please, let me hear your solution.'

'Very well,' Carmody said, and took a deep breath.

'The solution to your problem is inherent in the terms in which you view the problem. It could be no other way; every problem must contain within it the seeds of its own solution.'

'Must it?' Melichrone asked.

'Yes, it must,' Carmody said firmly.

'All right. For the moment I'll accept that premise. Go on.'

'Consider your situation,' Carmody said. 'Consider both its interior and exterior aspects. You are the God of this planet; but only of this planet. You are omnipotent and omniscient; but only here. You have impressive intellectual attainments, and you feel a call to serve something outside of yourself. But your gifts would be wasted any place but here, and here there is no one but you.'

'Yes, yes, that is exactly my situation!' Melichrone cried. 'But you still haven't told me what to do about it!'

Carmody took a deep breath and exhaled slowly. 'What you must do,' he said, 'is to use all of your great gifts, and to use them here, on your own planet, where they will be of maximum effect; and use them in the service of others, since this is your deepest desire.'

'In the service of others?' Melichrone asked.

'It is so indicated,' Carmody said. 'The most superficial consideration of your situation points the verdict. You are alone in a multiplex universe; but in order for you to perform exterior deeds, there must be an exterior. However, you are barred by your very essence from going to that exterior. Therefore the exterior must come to you. When it comes, what will be your relationship to it? That also is clear. Since you are omnipotent in your own world, you cannot be aided or assisted; but you can aid and assist others. This is the only natural relationship between you and the outside universe.'

Melichrone thought about it, then said, 'Your argument has force; that much I freely admit. But there are difficulties. For example, the outside world rarely comes this way. You are the first visitor I have had in two and a quarter galactic revolutions.'

'The job does require patience,' Carmody admitted. 'But patience is a quality you must strive for. It will be easier for you since time is a variable. And as for the number of your visitors – first of all, quantity does not affect quality. There is no value in mere enumeration. A man or a God does his job; that is what counts. Whether that job requires one or a million transactions makes no difference.'

'But I am as badly off as before if I have a job to perform and no one to perform it on.'

'With all modesty, I must point out that you have me,' Carmody said. 'I have come to you from the exterior. I have a problem; indeed, I have several problems. For me, these problems are insoluble. For you – I do not know. But I suspect that they will tax your powers to the utmost.'

Melichrone thought about it for a very long time. Carmody's nose began to itch, but he resisted the desire to scratch it. He waited, and the entire planet also waited while Melichrone made up his mind.

At last Melichrone raised his jet-black head and said, 'I really think you have something there!'

'It's good of you to say that,' Carmody said.

'But I mean it, I really do!' Melichrone said. 'Your solution seems to me both inevitable and elegant. And, by

53

extension, it seems to me that Fate, which rules men, Gods and planets, must have destined this to happen: that I, a creator, was created with no problem to solve; and that you, a created, became the creator of a problem that only a God could solve. And that you have lived out your lifetime waiting for me to solve your problem, while I have waited here for half of eternity for you to bring me your problem to solve!'

'I wouldn't be a bit surprised,' Carmody said. 'Would you like to know what my problem is?'

'I have already deduced,' Melichrone said. 'In fact, due to my superior intellect and experience, I know much more about it than you do. Superficially, your problem is how to get home.'

'That's it.'

'No, that's not it. I do not use words lightly. *Superficially*, you need to know Where, When and Which your planet is; and you need a way of getting there, and you need to arrive in much the same condition you are presently in. If that were all, it would still be difficult enough.'

'What else is there?' Carmody asked.

'Why, there is also the death which is pursuing you.'

'Oh,' Carmody said. He suddenly felt weak in the knees, and Melichrone graciously created an easy chair for him, and a Havana cigar, a Rum Collins, a pair of sheep-lined slippers, and a buffalo-hide lap robe.

'Comfortable?' Melichrone asked.

'Very.'

'Good. Pay close attention now. I will proceed to explain your situation briefly but succinctly, utilizing only a fraction of my intellect for that task while I use the rest of me for the considerable job of finding a feasible solution. But you will have to listen carefully and try to understand everything the first time I say it because we have very little time.'

'I thought you stretched my ten seconds into twenty-five years,' Carmody said.

'I did. But time is a tricky sort of variable, even for me. Eighteen of your twenty-five years are already used up, and the rest of them are going with extreme rapidity. Pay attention, now! Your life depends on it.'

'All right,' Carmody said. He sat forward and puffed on his cigar. 'I'm ready.'

'The first thing you must understand,' Melichrone said, 'is the nature of the implacable death that is hunting you.'

Carmody controlled a shudder and bent forward to listen.

Chapter 9

'The most fundamental fact in the Universe,' said Melichrone, 'is that species eat other species. It may not be pretty, but there it is. Eating is basic, and the acquisition of foodstuffs underlies all other phenomena. This concept involves the Law of Predation, which can be stated as follows: any given species, no matter how high or how low, feeds upon one or more species and is fed upon by one or more species.

'That sets forth a universal situation, which can be aggravated or ameliorated by a variety of circumstances. For example, a species resident in its own habitat can usually maintain itself in a state of Equilibrium, and thus live out its normal lifetime despite the depredations of predators. This Equilibrium is usually stated as the Victor-Vanquished equation, or VV. When a species or a species member moves to an alien and exotic habitat, the VV values necessarily change. Occasionally, there is temporary improvement in the species's Eat-Eaten Situation (Vv=Ee plus 1). More typically, there is a deterioration (Vv=Ee minus 1).

'That is what has happened to you, Carmody. You have left your normal habitat, which also means that you have left your normal predators. No automobiles can stalk you here, no virus can creep into your bloodstream, no policeman can shoot you down by mistake. You are separated from the dangers of Earth, and immune to the dangers of other galactic species.

'But the amelioration (Vv=Ee plus 1) is sadly temporary. The ironclad rule of Equilibrium has already begun to assert itself. You cannot refuse to hunt, and you cannot escape being hunted. Predation is Necessity itself.

'Having left Earth, you are a unique creature; therefore your predator is unique.

'Your predator was born out of a personification and solidification of universal law. This predator can feed exclusively and solely on you. The creature is shaped as a respondent and complement to your characteristics. Even without seeing it, we can know that its jaws are shaped to bite Carmodys, its limbs are articulated to seize and grasp Carmodys, its stomach has the peculiar and unique ability to digest Carmodys, and its personality is designed to take advantage of the Carmodic personality.

'Your situation has rendered you unique, Carmody; therefore your predator is unique. It is your death that pursues you, Carmody, and it does so with a desperation equal to your own. You and it are bound together. If it seizes you, you die; if you escape to the normal menaces of your own world, your predator dies for lack of Carmodic sustenance.

'There is no more I can say that will help you to evade it. I cannot predict the tricks and disguises it will attempt, no more than I can predict yours. I can only warn you that the probabilities always favour the Hunter, though escapes are not entirely unheard-of.

'That is the situation, Carmody. Have you understood me?'

Carmody started like a man awakened from a deep sleep.

'Yes,' he said. 'I don't understand everything you said. But I do understand the important parts.'

'Good,' Melichrone said. 'For we have no time left. You must leave this planet at once. Not even I on my own planet can arrest the universal Law of Predation.'

'Can you get me back to Earth?' Carmody asked.

'Given sufficient time, I probably could,' Melichrone said. 'But of course, given sufficient time, I could do anything at all. It is difficult, Carmody. To begin with, the three W variables must be solved each in terms of the other. I would have to determine exactly Where in space-time your planet is at the present moment; then I would have to discover Which of the alternate-probability Earths is yours. Then I would have to find the temporal sequence you were born into in order to determine When. Then

57

there is the skorish effect and the doubling factor, both of which must be allowed for. With all of that done, I could, with a little luck, slip you back into your own Particularity (a surprisingly delicate operation) without wrecking the whole works.'

'Can you do this for me?' Carmody asked.

'No. There is no time left. But I can send you to Maudsley, a friend of mine, who should be able to help you.'

'A friend of yours?'

'Well, perhaps not exactly a *friend*,' Melichrone said. 'More of an acquaintance, really. Though even that may be overstating the relationship. You see, once, quite some time ago, I almost left my planet for a sightseeing trip; and had I done so, I would have met Maudsley. But I didn't leave for various reasons, and therefore never actually met Maudsley. Still, we both know that if I had gone on my trip, we *would* have met, and would have exchanged views and outlooks, had an argument or two, cracked a few jokes, and ended with a mild fondness for each other.'

'It seems a kind of feeble relationship to presume upon,' Carmody said. 'Isn't there anyone else you could send me to?'

'I'm afraid not,' Melichrone said, 'Maudsley is my only friend. Probabilities define affinities just as well as actualities, you know. I'm sure Maudsley will take good care of you.'

'Well –' Carmody began to say. But then he noticed that something large and dark and menacing was beginning to take shape just behind his left shoulder, and he knew that he had used up all of his time.

'I'll go!' he said. 'And thanks for everything!'

'No need to thank me,' Melichrone said. 'My duty in the Universe is to serve strangers. Good luck, Carmody!'

The large menacing form was beginning to solidify; but before it could finish, Carmody had disappeared.

Chapter 10

Carmody found himself on a green meadow. It must have been noon, for a gleaming orange sun was directly over-head. Some distance away, a small herd of spotted cows grazed slowly over tall grass. Beyond them, Carmody could see a dark fringe of forest.

He turned around slowly. Meadowland extended on all sides of him, but the forest ended in dense under-brush. He heard a dog bark. There were mountains on the other side, a long, jagged range with snow-capped tops. Grey clouds clung to the upper slopes.

Out of the corner of his eye, he saw a flash of red. He turned; it seemed to be a fox. It looked at him curiously, then bounded away towards the forest.

'It's like Earth,' Carmody remarked. Then he remembered the Prize, which had last been a hibernating green snake. He felt around his neck, but the Prize was no long-er there.

'Here I am,' the Prize said.

Carmody looked around and saw a small copper caul-dron.

'Is this you?' Carmody asked, picking the cauldron up.

'Of course it's me,' the Prize said. 'Can't you even recognize your own Prize?'

'Well . . . you've changed quite a lot.'

'I am quite aware of that,' the Prize said. 'But my essence – the true me – never changes. What's the matter?'

Carmody had peered into the cauldron and had nearly dropped it. Inside, he had seen the skinned and half-consumed body of some small animal – perhaps a kitten.

'What's that inside you?' Carmody asked.

'It's my lunch, if you must know,' the Prize said. 'I was grabbing a quick bite during transit.'

'Oh.'

'Even Prizes need occasional nourishment,' the Prize added sarcastically. 'And, I might add, we also need rest, mild exercise, sexual congress, intermittent intoxication and an occasional bowel movement; none of which you have made provision for since I was awarded to you.'

'Well, I haven't had any of those things either,' Carmody answered.

'Do you really require them?' the Prize said in an astonished voice. 'Yes, of course, I suppose you do. It's strange, but I guess I had thought of you as a sort of bustling elemental figure without creature requirements.'

'Exactly the way I had thought of you!' Carmody said.

'It's inevitable, I suppose,' the Prize said. 'One tends to think of an alien as – as solid all through and *bowelless*, somehow. And of course, some aliens are.'

'I'll take care of your requirements,' Carmody said, feeling a sudden affection for his Prize. 'I'll do it as soon as this damned emergency is over.'

'Of course, old man. Forgive my fit of pique. D'ye mind if I finish my bite of lunch?'

'Go right ahead,' Carmody said. He was curious to see how a metal cauldron would devour a skinned animal; but when it came down to it, he was too squeamish to watch.

'Ah, that was damned good,' the Prize said. 'I've saved a bit for you, if you'd care for some.'

'I'm not too hungry just now,' Carmody said. 'What are you eating?'

'We call them *orithi*,' the Prize said. 'You would consider them a type of giant mushroom. Delicious raw or lightly poached in their own juices. The mottled white kind is better than the green.'

'I'll remember that,' Carmody said, 'in case I ever run across one. Do you think an Earthman could eat one?'

'I think so,' the Prize said. 'By the way, if you ever do get the chance, be sure to have it recite a poem before you eat it.'

'Why?'

'Because the *orithi* are very good poets.'

Carmody swallowed hard. That was the trouble with exotic life-forms; just when you thought you understood something, you found that you didn't understand at all. And conversely, when you thought you were completely mystified, they suddenly threw you off balance by acting in a completely comprehensible manner. In fact, Carmody decided, what made aliens so thoroughly alien was the fact that they weren't *completely* alien. It was amusing at first; but after a while it got on your nerves.

'Urp,' said the Prize.

'What?'

'I belched,' the Prize said. 'Excuse me. Anyhow, I think you must admit that I handled it all rather cleverly.'

'Handled all what?'

'The interview with Melichrone, of course,' said the Prize.

'You handled it? Why, damn it all, *you* were hibernating! *I* talked us out of that spot!'

'I don't want to contradict you,' the Prize said, 'but I fear that you are labouring under a misapprehension. I went into hibernation solely in order to bring all of my powers to bear on the problem of Melichrone.'

'You're crazy! You're out of your mind!' Carmody shouted.

'I am saying no more than the truth,' the Prize said. 'Consider that long, closely reasoned argument that you gave, in which you established Melichrone's place and function in the scheme of things by irrefutable logic.'

'What about it?'

'Well, have you ever reasoned that way before in your life? Are you a philosopher or a logician?'

'I was a philosophy major in college,' Carmody said.

'Big deal,' the Prize sneered. 'No, Carmody, you simply don't have the background or the intellect to handle an argument like that. Face it: it was completely out of character.'

'It was not out of character! I'm perfectly capable of extraordinary logic!'

'"Extraordinary" would be a good word for it,' the Prize said.

'But I did do it! I thought those thoughts!'

'Just as you wish,' the Prize said. 'I hadn't realized it

meant so much to you, and I certainly didn't mean to upset you. Tell me, have you ever been subject to fainting spells, or to inexplicable fits of laughter or tears?'

'No, I have not,' Carmody said, getting a grip on himself. 'Have you ever had recurrent dreams of flying, or sensations of saintliness?'

'I most certainly have not!' the Prize said.

'You're sure?'

'Sure, I'm sure!'

'Then we needn't discuss the matter any further,' Carmody said, feeling absurdly triumphant. 'But I'd like to know something else.'

'What is that?' the Prize said warily.

'What was Melichrone's disability that I was not supposed to mention? And what was his one limitation?'

'I thought that both were painfully obvious,' the Prize said.

'Not to me.'

'A few hours' reflection would bring them to your mind at once.'

'To hell with that,' Carmody said. 'Just tell me.'

'Very well,' the Prize said. 'Melichrone's one disability is that he is lame. It is a congenital defect; it has been present since his early origins. It persists throughout all his changes in analogous form.'

'And his one limitation?'

'He can never know about his own lameness. As a God, he is denied comparative knowledge. His creations are in his own image; which, in Melichrone's case, means that they are all lame. And his contacts with exterior reality are so few that he believes that lameness is the norm, and that unlame creatures are curiously flawed. Comparative knowledge is one of the few deficiencies of Godhead, by the way. Thus, the primary definition of a God is in terms of his self-sufficiency, which, no matter what its scope, is always interior. Perfect control of the controllable and perfect knowledge of the knowable are the first steps towards becoming a God, by the way, in case you ever wish to try the project.'

'Me? Try to be a God?'

'Why not?' the Prize asked him. 'It's an occupation like any other, despite its grand-sounding title. It's not easy, I'll grant you; but it's no harder than becoming a first-class poet or engineer.'

'I think you must be out of your mind,' Carmody said, feeling the quick shuddering shock of religious horror which so bedevils the atheistic.

'Not at all. I am merely better informed than you. But now you had better prepare yourself.'

Carmody looked around quickly and saw three small figures walking slowly across the meadow. Following them at a respectful distance were ten other figures.

'The one in the middle is Maudsley,' the Prize said. 'He's always very busy, but he may have time for a few words with you.'

'Does he have any limitations or defects?' Carmody said sarcastically.

'If he does, they are not of significance,' the Prize said. 'One deals with Maudsley in quite different terms, and faces entirely different problems.'

'He looks like a human,' Carmody said as the group came nearer.

'He is shaped like one,' the Prize admitted. 'But of course, the humanoid shape is common in this part of the galaxy.'

'What terms am I supposed to deal with him in?' Carmody asked.

'I can't really describe them,' the Prize said. 'Maudsley is too alien for me to understand or predict. But there *is* one piece of advice I can give you: be sure you get his attention and impress him with your humanity.'

'Well, of course,' Carmody said.

'It's not so simple as it sounds. Maudsley is an extremely busy being with a great deal on his mind. He is a highly gifted engineer, you know, and a dedicated one. But he tends to be absentminded, especially when he is trying out a new process.'

'Well, that doesn't sound too serious.'

'It's not – for Maudsley. It could be considered no more than an amusing foible, if it were not for the fact that he absentmindedly tends to view everything as raw material for his processes. An acquaintance of mine, Dewer Harding, came to him some time ago with an invitation to a party. Poor Dewer failed to capture his attention.'

'And what happened?'

'Maudsley processed him into one of his projects. Quite without malice, of course. Still, poor Dewer is now three pistons and a camshaft in a reciprocating engine, and can be seen weekdays in Maudsley's Museum of Historical Power Applications.'

'That's really quite shocking,' Carmody said. 'Can't anyone do anything about it?'

'No one wants to bring it to Maudsley's attention,' the

Prize said. 'Maudsley hates to admit an error and can be quite unpleasant if he feels he's being chivvied.'

The Prize must have perceived the look on Carmody's face, for he quickly added, 'But you mustn't let that alarm you! Maudsley is never vicious, and is in fact quite a good-hearted fellow. He likes praise, as do all of us; but he detests flattery. Just speak up and make yourself known, be admiring but avoid the fulsome, take exception to what you don't like, but don't be stubbornly critical; in short, exercise moderation except where a more extreme attitude is clearly called for.'

Carmody wanted to say that this advice was as good as no advice at all; worse, in fact, since it merely served to make him nervous. But now there was no time. Maudsley was here, tall and white-haired, in chinos and a leather jacket, flanked by two men in business suits with whom he was talking vehemently.

'Good day, sir,' Carmody said firmly. He stepped forward, then scuttled out of the way before the oblivious trio ran into him.

'A bad beginning,' the Prize whispered.

'Shut up,' Carmody whispered back. With a certain grimness, he hurried after the group.

Chapter 11

'So this is it, eh, Orin?' Maudsley said.

'Yes sir, this is it,' Orin, the man on his left said, smiling proudly. 'What do you think of it, sir?'

Maudsley turned around slowly and surveyed the meadow, the mountains, the sun, the river, the forest. His face betrayed no expression. He said, 'What do *you* think of it, Brookside?'

Brookside said, in a tremulous voice, 'Well, sir, I think that Orin and I did a nice job. A *really* nice job, if you take into account that it was our first independent project.'

'And do you concur in that judgement, Orin?' Maudsley asked.

'Certainly, sir,' Orin said.

Maudsley bent down and plucked a blade of grass. He sniffed it and threw it away. He scuffed the dirt beneath his feet, then stared for several moments full into the blazing sun. In a measured voice, he said, 'I am amazed, truly amazed. But in a most unpleasant way. I ask you two to build a world for one of my customers and you come up with *this*! Do you really consider yourselves engineers?'

The two aides did not reply. They had stiffened, like boys awaiting the birch rod.

'Engineers!' Maudsley said, getting almost fifty foot-pounds of contempt into the word. '"Creative but practical scientists who can build the planet where and when you want it." Do either of you recognize those words?'

'They're from the standard brochure,' Orin said.

'That is correct,' Maudsley said. 'Now, do you consider *this* a good example of "creative, practical engineering"?'

Both men were silent. Then Brookside blurted out, 'Well sir, yes sir, I do!

'We examined the job specs very carefully. The request was for a Type 34Bc4 planet with certain variations. And that's exactly what we built. This is only a corner of it, of course. But still –'

'But still, I can see what you did and judge accordingly,' Maudsley said. 'Orin! What kind of a heating unit did you use?'

'A type O5 sun, sir,' Orin replied. 'It fitted the thermal requirements nicely.'

'I daresay it did. But this was a budget world, you will remember. If we don't keep the costs down, we don't make a profit. And the biggest single cost item is the heating unit.'

'We are aware of that, sir,' Brookside said. 'We didn't at all like to use an O5-type sun for a single-planet system. But the heat and radiation requirements –'

'Haven't you learned anything from me?' Maudsley cried. 'This type of star is entirely superfluous. You there –' He beckoned to the workmen. 'Take it down.'

The workmen hurried forward with a folding ladder. One man braced it and another man unfolded it, ten times, a hundred times, a million times. Two other workmen raced up the ladder as fast as it went up.

'Handle it carefully!' Maudsley called up to them. 'And be sure you're wearing gloves! That thing's hot!'

The workmen at the very top of the ladder unhooked the star, folded it into itself and put it into a padded box marked ' STAR: HANDLE WITH CARE.'

When the lid fell, everything went black.

'Hasn't anyone any sense around here?' Maudsley asked. 'Damn it all, let there be light.'

And just like that, there was light.

'OK,' Maudsley said. 'That O5-type sun goes back into storage. On a job like this we can use a G13-type star.'

'But sir,' Orin said nervously, 'it isn't hot enough.'

'I know that,' Maudsley said. 'That's where you have to use your creativity. If you move the star closer in, it'll be hot enough.'

'Yes sir, it will,' Brookside said, 'but it'll be emitting PR rays without enough space to allow them to dissipate harmlessly. And that might kill off the entire race that's going to occupy this planet.'

Maudsley said, very slowly and distinctly, 'Are you trying to tell me that G13-type stars are dangerous?'

'Well, no, I didn't mean it exactly *that* way,' Orin said. 'I meant to say, they *can* be dangerous, just like anything else in the universe, if proper precautions are not taken.'

'That's more like it,' Maudsley said.

'The proper precautions,' Brookside said, 'involve, in this case, the wearing of protective lead suits weighing some fifty pounds each. But this is impractical, since the average member of this race only weighs eight pounds.'

'That's their lookout,' Maudsley said. 'It's not our business to tell them how to live their lives. Am I supposed to be responsible whenever they stub their toe on a rock I put on their planet? Besides, they don't have to wear lead suits. They can buy one of my optional extras, a solar screen that'll block out the PR rays.'

Both men smiled nervously. But Orin said timidly, 'I believe this is a somewhat underprivileged species, sir. I think perhaps they can't afford the solar screen.'

'Well, if not right now, maybe later,' Maudsley said. 'And anyhow, the PR radiations aren't instantly fatal. Even with it, they'll have an average lifespan of 9·3 years, which ought to be enough for anyone.'

'Yes sir,' the two assistant engineers said, not happily.

'Next,' Maudsley said, 'what's the height of those mountains?'

'They average six thousand feet above sea level,' Brookside said.

'At least three thousand feet too high,' Maudsley said. 'Do you think mountains grow on trees? Pare them down and put what you have left over into the warehouse.'

Brookside took out a notebook and jotted down the change. Maudsley continued to pace around, looking and frowning.

'How long are those trees supposed to last?'

'Eight hundred years, sir. They're the new improved model Appleoak. They give fruit, shade, nuts, refreshing beverages, three useful fabrics, they make excellent building material, hold the soil in place, and –'

'Are you trying to bankrupt me?' Maudsley roared. 'Two hundred years is entirely long enough for a tree! Drain off most of their *élan vital* and store it in the life-force accumulator!'

'They won't be able to perform all of their designed functions, then,' Orin said.

'Then cut down on their functions! Shade and nuts is plenty, we don't have to make a damned treasure chest out of those trees! Now then, who put those cows out there?'

'I did, sir,' Brookside said. 'I thought it would make the place look – well, sort of inviting, sir.'

'You oaf,' Maudsley said. 'The time to make a place look inviting is before the sale, not after! This place was sold unfurnished. Put those cows into the protoplasm vat.'

'Yes, sir,' Orin said. 'Terribly sorry, sir. Is there anything else?'

'There's about ten thousand other things wrong,' Maudsley said. 'But you can figure out those for yourselves, I hope. What, for example, is this?' He pointed at Carmody. 'A statue or something? Is he supposed to sing a song or recite a poem when the new race arrives?'

Carmody said, 'Sir, I am not part of this. A friend of yours named Melichrone sent me, and I'm trying to get home to my own planet –'

Maudsley clearly did not hear what Carmody was saying. For, while Carmody was trying to speak, Maudsley was saying, 'Whatever he is, the job specs don't call for him. So stick him back in the protoplasm vat with the cows.'

'Hey!' Carmody shouted as workmen lifted him up by his arms. 'Hey, wait a minute!' he screamed. 'I'm not a part of this planet! Melichrone sent me! Wait, hold on, listen to me!'

'You really ought to be ashamed of yourselves,' Maudsley went on, oblivious to Carmody's shrieks. 'What was that supposed to be? One of your interior decorating touches, Orin?'

'Oh no,' Orin said. 'I didn't put him there.'

'Then it was you, Brookside.'

'I never saw him before in my life, chief.'

'Hmm,' Maudsley said. 'You're both fools, but you've never been liars. Hey!' he shouted to the workmen. 'Bring him back here!

'All right, pull yourself together,' Maudsley said to Carmody, who was shaking uncontrollably. 'Get a grip on yourself, I can't wait around here while you have a fit of hysterics! Better now? All right, would you mind explaining just what you're doing trespassing on my property and why I shouldn't have you converted into protoplasm?'

Chapter 12

'I see,' Maudsley said, after Carmody had finished explaining. 'It's an interesting story, though I'm sure you've overdramatized it. Still, here you are, and you're looking for a planet called – Earth?'

'That is correct, sir,' Carmody said.

'Earth,' Maudsley mused, scratching his head. 'This is most fortunate for you; I seem to remember the place.'

'Do you really, Mr Maudsley?'

'Yes, I'm quite sure of it,' Maudsley said. 'It's a small green planet, and it supports a monomorphic humanoid race like yourself. Am I right?'

'Completely right!' Carmody said.

'I have rather a memory for these things,' Maudsley said. 'And in this particular case, as at happens, I built Earth.'

'Did you really, sir?' Carmody asked.

'Yep. I remember distinctly, because in the course of building it, I also invented science. Perhaps you will find the story amusing.' He turned to his aides. 'And *you* might find the tale instructive.'

No one was going to deny Maudsley the right to tell a story. So Carmody and the assistant engineers assumed attentive postures, and Maudsley began.

The Story of the Creation of Earth

I was still quite a small contractor then. I put up a planet here and there, and I got to do an occasional dwarf star. But jobs were always hard to come by, and the customers were invariably capricious, fault-finding, and slow in their payments. Customers were hard to please in those days; they argued about every little detail. *Change this, change that, why must water flow downhill, the gravity's too heavy, the hot air rises when it ought to fall.* And so forth.

I was quite naïve in those days. I used to explain the aesthetic and practical reasons for everything I did. Before long, the questions and the explanations were taking longer than the jobs. There was entirely too much talk-talk. I knew that I had to do something about it, but I couldn't figure out what.

Then, just before the Earth project, a whole new approach to customers' relations began to shape itself in my mind. I found myself muttering to myself, 'Form follows function.' I liked the way it sounded. But then I would ask myself, '*Why* must form follow function?' And the reason I gave myself was, 'Form follows function because that is an immutable law of nature and one of the fundamental axioms of applied science.' And I liked the sound of that, too, although it didn't make much sense.

But sense didn't matter. What mattered was that I had made a new discovery. I had unwittingly stumbled into the art of advertising and salesmanship, and I had discovered the gimmick of great possibilities, namely, the doctrine of scientific determinism.

Earth was my first test case, and that is why I will always remember it.

A tall, bearded old man with piercing eyes had come to me and ordered a planet. (That was how your planet began, Carmody.) Well, I did the job quickly, in six days I believe, and thought that would be the end of it. It was another of those budget planets, and I had cut a few corners here and there. But to hear the owner complain, you'd have thought I'd stolen the eyes out of his head.

'Why are there so many tornadoes?' he asked. 'It's part of the atmosphere circulation system,' I told him. (Actually, I had been a little rushed at that time; I had forgotten to put in an air-circulation overload valve.)

'Three-quarters of the place is water!' he told me. 'And I clearly specified a four-to-one land-to-water ratio!'

'Well, we couldn't do it that way!' I told him. (I had lost his ridiculous specifications; I never can keep track of these absurd little one-planet projects.)

'And you've filled what little land you gave me with deserts and swamps and jungles and mountains.'

'It's scenic,' I pointed out.

'I don't care from scenic!' the fellow thundered. 'Oh, sure, one ocean, a dozen lakes, a couple rivers, one or two mountain ranges, that would have been fine. Dresses the place up, gives the inhabitants a good feeling. But what you gave me is *shlock!*'

'There's a reason for it,' I said. (In point of fact, we couldn't make the job pay except by using reconstituted mountains, a lot of rivers and oceans as filler, and a couple of deserts I had bought cheap from Ourie the Planet-Junker. But I wasn't going to tell *him* that.)

'A reason!' he screamed. 'What will I tell my people? I'm putting an entire race on that planet, maybe two or three. They'll be humans, made in my own image; and humans are notoriously picky, just as I am. What am I supposed to tell them?'

Well, I knew what he could tell them; but I didn't want to be offensive, so I pretended to give the matter some thought. And strangely enough, I *did* think. And I came up with the gimmick to end all gimmicks.

'You just tell them the plain scientific truth,' I said. 'You tell them that, scientifically, everything that *is* must be.'

'Huh?' he said.

'It's determinism,' I said, making up the name on the spur of the moment. 'It's quite simple, though a bit esoteric. To start with, form follows function; therefore your planet is exactly as it should be by the simple fact of *being* at all. Next, science is invariable; so if anything isn't invariable, it ain't science. And finally, everything follows definite rules. You can't always figure out what those rules are, but you can be sure they're there. So, it stands to reason that no one ought to ask *why this instead of that?* Instead, everyone ought to ask *how does it work?*'

Well, he asked me some pretty tough questions, and he was a pretty smart old fellow. But he didn't know damn-all about engineering; his field was ethics and morals and religion and spook stuff like that. So of course, he just wasn't able to come up with any real objections. He was one of these types who love abstractions, and he started repeating, '"That which *is* is that which *must be.*" Hmm, a very intriguing formula and not without its patina of stoicism. I shall incorporate some of these insights into the lessons I give to my people . . . But tell me this: how can I reconcile this indeterminate fatality of science with the free will I plan to give to my people?'

Well, the old boy almost had me there. I smiled and coughed to give myself time to think, and then I said, 'The answer is obvious!' Which is always a good answer, as far as it goes.

'I daresay it is,' he said. 'But I don't perceive it.'

'Look,' I said, 'this free will you're giving your people, isn't that a kind of fatality also?'

'It could be considered as such. But the difference –'

'And besides,' I said hastily, 'since when are free will and fatality incompatible?'

'They certainly seem incompatible,' he said.

'That's only because you don't understand science,' I said, performing the old switcheroo right under his hooked nose. 'You see, my dear sir, one of the most basic laws of science is that chance plays a part in everything. Chance, I'm sure you know, is the mathematical equivalent of free will.'

'But what you're saying is quite contradictory,' he said.

'That's how it goes,' I said. 'Contradiction is one more of the fundamental rules of the Universe. Contradiction generates strife, without which everything would reach a stage of entropy. So we couldn't have any planet or any universe if things didn't exist in an apparently irreconcilable state of contradiction.'

'Apparently?' he said, quick as a flash.

'Right as rain,' I said. 'Contradiction, which we can define provisionally as the existence of reality-paired opposites, isn't the last word on the subject. For example, let's posit a single isolated tendency. What happens when you push a tendency to the limit?'

'I haven't the slightest idea,' the old guy said. 'The lack of specifics in this sort of discussion –'

'What happens,' I said, 'is that the tendency turns into its *opposite*.'

'Does it really?' he asked, considerably shook up. These religious types are something when they try to tackle science.

'It really does,' I assured him. 'I've got the proofs in my lab, though the demonstrations are a bit tedious –'

'No, please, I take your word,' the old guy said. 'After all, we did make a Covenant.'

That was the word he always used for 'contract.' It meant the same thing, but sounded better.

'Paired opposites,' he mused. 'Determinism. Things becoming their opposites. It's all quite intricate, I'm afraid.'

'And aesthetic as well,' I said. 'But I didn't finish about the transformation of extremes.'

'Kindly go on,' he said.

'Thanks. Now then, we have entropy, which means that things persist in their motion unless there is outside influence. (Sometimes even when there is outside influence, in my experience.) But so, we got entropy driving a thing towards its opposite. If one thing is driven towards its opposite, then all things are driven towards their opposite, because science is consistent. Now you get the picture? We've got all these opposites transforming themselves like crazy and becoming their opposites. On a higher level of organization, we have groups of opposites going through the same bit. And higher and higher. So far so good?'

'I suppose so,' he said.

'Fine. Now, the question naturally arises, is this *all*? I mean, these opposites turning themselves inside out and then outside in, is that the whole ball game? And the beauty part is, it's not! No, sir. These opposites flipping around like trained seals are only an aspect of what's really happening. Because –' And here I paused and spoke in a very deep voice. ' – because there is a wisdom that sees beyond the clash and turmoil of the phenomenal world. This wisdom, sir, sees through the illusory quality of these real things, and sees beyond them into the deeper workings of the Universe, which are in a state of like great and magnificent harmony.'

'How can a thing be both illusory and real?' he asked me, quick as a whip.

'It is not for me to know an answer like that,' I told him. 'Me, I am a mere humble scientific worker and I see what I see and act accordingly. But maybe there's an ethical reason behind it.'

The old boy mused on that one for a while, and I could see he was having quite a tussle with himself. He could detect a logical fallacy as fast as anyone, of course, and my reasons had been shot through with them. But like all eggheads, he was fascinated with contradictions and he had the strong urge to incorporate them into his system. And all the propositions I had proposed, well, his common sense told him that things couldn't be *that* tricky; but his intellectuality told him that maybe things did indeed seem that complicated, but maybe there was a nice simple unifying principle underneath it all. Or, if not a unifying principle, at least a good solid moral. And finally, I had hooked him all over again just because I had used the word 'ethics.' Because this old gent was a perfect demon for ethics, he was supersaturated with ethics; you could call him Mr Ethics, make no mistake. And so, quite accidentally, I had given him the idea that the whole bloody Universe was a series of homilies and contradictions, of laws and inequities, all leading to the most exquisite and rarefied sort of ethical order.

'There is a greater depth here than I had considered,' he said after a while. 'I had planned to instruct my people in ethics only; and to direct their attention to morally imperative questions such as how and why a man should live instead of what constitutes living matter; I wanted them to be explorers plumbing the depths of joy, fear, piety, hope, despair, rather than scientists who examine stars and raindrops and form grandiose and impractical hypotheses on the basis of their findings. I was aware of the Universe, but considered it superfluous. Now you have corrected me.'

'Well, look,' I said, 'I didn't mean to cause trouble. I just thought I should point out this stuff . . .'

The old man smiled. 'By causing me trouble,' he said, 'you have spared me greater trouble. I can create in my own image; but I will not create a world peopled with miniature versions of myself. Free will is important to me. My creatures will have it, to their glory and their sorrow. They will take this glittering useless toy which you call science and they will elevate it to an undeclared Godhead. Physical contradictions and solar abstractions will fascinate them; they will pursue knowledge of these things and forget to explore the knowledge of their own heart. You have convinced me of this, and I am grateful for the forewarning.'

I'll be frank, he got me a little nervous just about then. I mean, he was a nobody, he didn't know any important people; and yet, he had the grand manner. I had the feeling that he could cause me one hell of a lot of trouble, and I felt that he could do it with a few words, a sentence like a poisoned dart lodged in my mind and never to be removed. And that scared me a little, to tell the truth.

Well sir, the old joker must have been reading my mind. For he said, 'Do not be frightened. I accept without reservation the world you have built for me; it will serve very well, exactly as it is. As for the flaws and defects which you also built into my world, I accept those also, not entirely without gratitude; and I pay for those, too.'

'How?' I asked. 'How do you pay for errors?'

'By accepting them without dispute,' he said. 'And by turning away from you now and going about my business and the business of my people.'

And the old gentleman left without another word.

'Well, it left me pretty thoughtful. I'd had all the good arguments, but the old boy left somehow with the last word. I knew what he meant; he had fulfilled his contract with me and that ended it. He was leaving with no word for me personally. From his point of view, it was a kind of punishment.

'But that's only the way *he* saw it. What did I need with his word? I wanted to hear it, of course; that's only natural; and for quite a while I tried to look him up. But he didn't care to see me.

'So it really doesn't matter. I made a pretty nice profit on that world, and even if I bent the contract here and there, I didn't break it. That's how things are; you owe it to yourself to make a profit. You can't get too worked up over the consequences.

'But I was trying to make a point out of all this, and I want you boys to listen carefully. Science is filled with a lot of rules, because I invented it that way. Why did I invent it that way? Because rules are a great assistance to a smart operator, just as a lot of laws are a great help to lawyers. The rules, doctrines, axioms, laws, and principles of science are there to help you, not to hinder you. They're there in order to provide you with reasons for what you do. Most of them are true, more or less, and that helps.

'But always remember – these rules are there to help you explain to the customers what you do *after you do it*, not before. When you have a project, do it exactly as you see fit; then fit the facts around the event, not the other way around.

'Remember – these rules exist as a verbal barrier against people who ask questions. But they should *not* be used as a barrier by you. If you've learned anything from me, you've learned that our work is inevitably inexplicable; we simply do it, and sometimes it comes out well and sometimes not.

'But never try to explain to yourselves why some things happen and why other things don't happen. Don't ask, and don't imagine that an explanation exists. Get me?'

The two assistants nodded vehemently. They looked enlightened, like men who have found a new religion. Carmody would have bet anything that those two earnest young men had memorized every one of the Builder's words, and would now proceed to elevate those words into – a rule.

Chapter 13

After finishing his story, Maudsley was silent for a long time. He seemed morose and withdrawn, and filled with unhappy thoughts. But after a while he roused himself and said, 'Carmody, a person in my position is always beset by requests from various charities. I give generously every year to the Oxygen Fund for Indigent Carbon-Forms. I also contribute to the Interstellar Redevelopment Foundation, the Cosmic Settlement Home, and the Save-the-Immature programme. This seems to me quite sufficient, and is also tax-deductible.'

'All right,' Carmody said, with a sudden flash of pride. 'I don't want your charity anyhow.'

'Please do not interrupt me,' Maudsley said. 'I was saying that my charities are quite sufficient to fulfil my humanitarian instincts. I do not like to take up individual cases because it gets messy and personal.'

'I quite understand,' Carmody said. 'I think I had better go now,' he added, though he didn't have the slightest idea of where he was going or how he would get there.

'I asked you not to interrupt me,' Maudsley said. 'Now, I don't like to take personal cases, as I said. But I am going to make an exception this time and help you get back to your planet.'

'Why?' Carmody asked.

'A whim,' Maudsley said. 'The merest fancy, with perhaps a touch of altruism thrown in. Also –'

'Yes?'

'Well, if you ever get home – which is dubious in spite of my help – I would appreciate your delivering a message.'

'Sure,' Carmody said. 'Who's the message to?'

'Why, obviously, to the bearded old man for whom I built the planet. I suppose he's still in charge?'

'I don't know,' Carmody said. 'There's been a great deal of discussion on that point. Some people say he's there just as he always has been. But others say he's dead (though I think that's meant metaphorically), and still others maintain that he never existed in the first place.'

'He's still there,' Maudsley said with conviction. 'You couldn't kill a fellow like that with a crowbar. As for his apparent absence, that's very like him. He's moody, you know, and filled with high morals which he expects people to live by. He can be peevish, he can just drop out of sight for a while if he doesn't like how things are going. And he can be subtle; he knows that people don't like too much of anything, no matter if it's roast beef, lovely women, or God. So it would be just like him to remove himself from the bill of fare, so to speak, until an appetite has been built up for him again.'

'You seem to know a lot about him,' Carmody said.

'Well, I've had a lot of time to think about him.'

'And I think that I should point out,' Carmody pointed out, 'that the way you see him is not in accord with any theological view that I've ever heard. The idea that God can be moody, peevish –'

'But he must be those things,' Maudsley said. 'And much more besides! He must be a creature of extreme emotionality! After all, that's how *you* are and, I presume, how your fellow humans are.'

Carmody nodded.

'Well, there you are! He stated plainly that he was going to create in his own image. And obviously, he did so. The moment you came here, I recognized the family resemblance. There is a little God in you, Carmody, though you shouldn't let that go to your head.'

'I've never had any contact with him,' Carmody said. 'I don't know how to give him a message.'

'It's so plain!' Maudsley said, with an air of exasperation. 'When you get home, you must simply speak up in a firm, clear voice.'

'What makes you think he'll hear me?' Carmody asked.

'He can't help but hear you!' Maudsley said. 'It *is* his planet, you know, and he has shown his deep interest in his tenants. If he had wanted you to communicate in any other way, he would have shown it.'

'All right, I'll do it,' Carmody said. 'What do you want me to tell him?'

'Well, it isn't anything much, really,' Maudsley said, suddenly ill at ease. 'But he was quite a worthy old gentleman, really, and I've felt a bit bad about the planet I built him. Not that there's anything *wrong* with the planet, when you come right down to it. It's quite serviceable and all that. But this old guy was a gentleman. I mean, he had class, which is something you never see too much of. So I'd kind of like to do a renovation on that planet of his, entirely free you understand, gratis, it wouldn't cost him a cent. If he'd go for it, I could turn that planet into a showplace, a real paradise. I'm really a hell of a good engineer, let me tell you; it's quite unfair to judge me by the borax I have to turn out to earn a buck.'

'I'll tell him,' Carmody said. 'But very frankly, I don't think he'll take you up on the offer.'

'I don't think he will, either,' Maudsley said morosely. 'He's a stubborn old man and he doesn't want favours from anyone. Still, I do want to make the offer, and I mean it in all sincerity.' Maudsley hesitated, then said, 'You might also ask him if he'd care to drop around for a chat sometime.'

'Why don't you go to see him?'

'I tried that a couple of times, but he wouldn't see me. He's got quite a vindictive streak, that old man of yours! Still, maybe he'll relent.'

'Maybe,' Carmody said doubtfully. 'Anyhow, I'll tell him. But if you want to talk to a God, Mr Maudsley, why don't you talk to Melichrone?'

Maudsley threw back his head and laughed. 'Melichrone! That imbecile? He's a pompous, self-centred ass, and he has no character worth considering. I'd rather talk metaphysics with a dog! Technically speaking, Godhead is a matter of power and control, you know; there's nothing magical about it, and it's not a cure-all for what ails you. No two Gods are alike. Did you know that?'

'No, I didn't.'

'Bear it in mind. You can never tell when a piece of information like that will prove useful.'

'Thank you,' Carmody said. 'You know, before this, I didn't believe in any God at all.'

Maudsley looked thoughtful and said, 'To my way of thinking, the existence of a God or Gods is obvious and inevitable; and belief in God is as easy and natural as belief in an apple, and of no more or less significance. When you come right down to it, there's only one thing that stands in the way of this belief.'

'What's that?' Carmody asked.

'It is the Principle of Business, which is more fundamental than the law of gravity. Wherever you go in the galaxy, you can find a food business, a house-building business, a war business, a peace business, a governing business, and so forth. And, of course, a God business, which is called "religion," and which is a particularly reprehensible line of endeavour. I could talk for a year on the perverse and nasty notions that the religions sell, but I'm sure you've heard it all before. But I'll just mention one matter, which seems to underlie everything the religions preach, and which seems to me almost exquisitely perverse.'

'What's that?' Carmody asked.

'It's the deep, fundamental bedrock of hypocrisy upon which religion is founded. Consider: no creature can be said to worship if it does not possess free will. Free will, however, is *free*. And just by virtue of being free, is intractable and incalculable, a truly Godlike gift, the faculty that makes a state of freedom possible. To exist in a state of freedom is a wild, strange thing, and was clearly intended as such. But what do the religions do with this? They say, "Very well, you possess free will; but now you must use your free will to enslave yourself to God and to us." The effrontery of it! God, who would not coerce a fly, is painted as a supreme slavemaster! In the face of this, any creature with spirit must rebel, must serve God entirely of his own will and volition, or must not serve him at all, thus remaining true to himself and to the faculties God has given him.'

'I think I see what you mean,' Carmody said.

'I've made it too complicated,' Maudsley said. 'There's a much simpler reason for avoiding religion.'

'What's that?'

'Just consider its style – bombastic, hortatory, sickly-sweet, patronizing, artificial, inapropos, boring, filled with dreary images or peppy slogans – fit subject matter for senile old women and unweaned babies, but for no one else. I cannot believe that the God I met here would ever enter a church; he had too much taste and ferocity, too much anger and pride. I can't believe it, and for me that ends the matter. Why should I go to a place that a God would not enter?'

Chapter 14

Carmody was left to his own devices while Maudsley began construction of a machine to take him back to Earth. He became very bored. Maudsley could only work in utter solitude, and the Prize had apparently gone back into hibernation. Orin and Brookside, the junior engineers, were dull fellows, preoccupied with their work and uninterested in anything else. So Carmody had no one to talk to.

He filled in his time as well as he could. He toured an atom-building factory and listened dutifully while a red-faced foreman explained how it was done.

'This used to be all handwork,' the foreman told him. 'Now machines do it, but the process is really the same. First, we select a proton and attach a neutron to it, using Mr Maudsley's patented energy-binding. Then, we spin the electrons into position with a standard microcosmic centrifuge. After that, we put in anything else that's called for – mu mesons, positrons, that sort of gingerbread. And that's all there is to it.'

'Do you get much call for gold or uranium atoms?' Carmody asked.

'Not much. Too expensive. Mostly, we turn out hydrogen atoms.'

'What about antimatter atoms?'

'I've never seen much sense in it, myself,' the foreman said. 'But Mr Maudsley carries it as a sideline. Antimatter is made in a separate factory, of course.'

'Of course,' Carmody said.

'That stuff explodes when it comes into contact with normal atoms.'

'Yes, I know. It must be tricky stuff to package.'

'No, not really,' the foreman assured him. 'We put it up in neutral cartons.'

They continued to walk among the huge machines, and Carmody tried to think of something else to say. Finally he asked, 'Do you make your own protons and electrons?'

'Nope, Mr Maudsley never wanted to fool around with that really small stuff. We get our subatomic particles from subcontractors.'

Carmody laughed and the foreman looked at him suspiciously. They continued to walk until Carmody's feet began to hurt him.

He felt tired and dull, and this annoyed him. He ought to be fascinated, he told himself. Here he was, in a place that actually manufactured atoms, and had separate facilities for creating antimatter! Over there was a gigantic machine that extracted cosmic rays from raw space, and purified them, and bottled them in heavy green containers. Beyond that was a thermal probe, used for doctoring up old stars; and just to the left of it . . .

It was no use. Walking through Maudsley's factory elicited in Carmody the same sensations of boredom he had experienced during a guided tour through a Gary, Indiana, steel foundry. And that wave of sullen fatigue, that sense of mute rebellion – he had felt just the same after walking for reverent hours through the hushed corridors of the Louvre, the Prado, the British Museum. One's sense of wonder, he realized, is only capable of a small amount of appreciation. Men remain inexorably true to themselves and their interests. They stay in character, even if that character is suddenly transported to Timbuktu or Alpha Centauri. And, being ruthlessly honest about it, Carmody realized that he would rather ski the Nosedive at Stowe or sail a Tahiti ketch beneath Hell Gate Bridge than see most of the marvels of the Universe. He was ashamed of this, but there wasn't much he could do about it.

'I guess I'm just not particularly Faustian,' he said to himself. 'Here are the secrets of the Universe spread around me like old newspapers, and I'm dreaming about a nice February morning in Vermont before the snow has got carved up.'

He felt bad for a while, but then he began to feel rebellious: 'After all, not even Faust had to walk through this stuff like it was an exhibition of Old Masters. He had to work his ass off, if I remember correctly. If the devil had made it too easy for him, Faust would have probably given up knowledge and taken up mountain-climbing or something.'

He thought for a while. Then he said, 'Anyhow. What's such a big deal about the secrets of the Universe? They've been overrated, just like everything else. When you come right down to it, nothing's as good as you think it's going to be.'

All of that, even if it were not true, at least served to make Carmody feel better. But he was still bored. And Maudsley still did not come out of his seclusion.

* * *

Time passed with apparent slowness. It was impossible to judge its true rate; but Carmody had the impression that it dragged on and on, and could have been subdivided into days and weeks, perhaps even a month. He also had the feeling – or the premonition – that Maudsley was not finding it easy to do what he had promised so lightly. Perhaps it was simpler to build a new planet than to find an old one. Becoming aware of the complexity of the task and its many unexpected dimensions, Carmody grew disheartened.

One day (to speak conventionally) he watched Orin and Brookside construct a forest. It had been ordered by the primates of Coeth II, to replace their old forest, which had been struck by a meteor. This new one had been paid for entirely out of schoolchildren's donations; a sufficient sum had been raised to purchase a first-class job.

When the engineers and workmen had left, Carmody wandered alone through the trees. He marvelled at how good a job Maudsley and his team could do when they put their minds to it, for this forest was a marvel of creative and considerate planning.

There were natural glades for walking, with a leafy arbour above and a springy, dappled loam below – enticing to the foot and restful to the eye. The trees were not Earth species, but they were similar. So Carmody chose to ignore the differences and name them after the trees he had known.

That forest was all prime first-growth timberland, with just enough underbrush to keep it interesting. It was landscaped here and there with bright, rushing streams, none deeper than three feet. There was a shallow, intensely blue little lake, flanked by ponderosa pine or its equivalent. And there was a miniature swamp, dense with mangrove and cypress, studded with blackgums, magnolias and willows, and liberally sprinkled coconut palms. Farther back from the water's edge, on drier land, was a grove in which could be found wild plum and cherry trees, and chestnuts, pecans, oranges, persimmons, dates and figs. It was a perfect place for a picnic.

Nor had the arboreal potentialities of the forest been overlooked. The young primates could race up and down the straight-backed elms and sycamores, play follow-the-leader in the many-branched oaks and laurels, or teeter precariously across the tangled network of vines and creepers that interconnected the treetops. Nor had the needs of their elders been ignored; there were giant redwoods for them, where they could doze or play cards, high above the screaming children.

But there was much more than this; even an untrained person like Carmody could see that the little forest had been given a simple, pleasant and purposeful ecology. There were birds, animals, and other creatures. There were flowers, and stingless bees to cross-fertilize them and gather the pollen, and jolly fat little bears to steal the bees' honey. There were grubs to feast on the flowers, and bright-winged birds to feast off the grubs, and quick red foxes to eat the birds, and bears to eat the foxes, and primates to eat the bears.

But the primates of Coeth also die, and are buried in the forest in shallow, coffinless graves, reverently but without undue fuss, and are fed upon by grubs, birds, foxes, bears and even one or two species of flowers. In this way the Coethians have an integral place in the forest cycle of life and death; and this pleases them very much since they are born participants.

Carmody observed all of this, walking alone with the Prize (still a cauldron) under his arm, and thinking tremulous thoughts about his lost homeland. Then he heard a branch rustle behind him.

There was no wind, and the bears were all bathing in the pond. Carmody turned around slowly, knowing something was there but wishing it weren't.

There was indeed something there. There was a creature wearing a bulky, grey plastic space suit, Frankenstein-type shoes, a transparent bubble helmet and a belt from which dangled a dozen or more tools, weapons and instruments.

Carmody immediately recognized this apparition as an Earthman; no other creature could dress that way.

Behind and to the right of the Earthman was a slighter, similarly clad figure. Carmody saw at once that this was an Earthwoman, and a very attractive one.

'Good lord!' Carmody said. 'How did you people happen to come here, of all places?'

'Not so loud,' the Earthman said. 'I just thank God we arrived in time. But now, I'm afraid, the most dangerous part is ahead of us.'

'Do we have any chance at all, Father?' the girl asked.

'There is always a chance,' the man said, with a grim smile. 'But I wouldn't bet any money on it. Still, maybe Dr Maddox can figure something out.'

'He's very good at that, isn't he, Dad?' the girl asked.

'Sure he is, Mary,' the man replied in a gentle voice. 'Doc Maddox is the finest there ever was. But he – all of us – may have overreached ourselves this time.'

'I'm sure we'll find a way,' the girl said, with heart-breaking serenity.

'Maybe,' the man said. 'Anyhow, we'll show 'em there's still a few pounds of thrust in the old brain-jets.' He turned to Carmody, and his expression hardened. 'I just hope you're worth it, Mac,' he said. 'Three lives are going on the line for you.'

It was a difficult proposition to respond to, and Carmody didn't even try.

'Single file quick-step back to the ship,' the man said. 'We'll get Doc Maddox's assessment of the situation.'

Drawing a bulb-nosed gun from his belt, the man turned into the woods. The girl followed, giving Carmody an encouraging look over her shoulder. Carmody fell into line behind her.

Chapter 15

'Hey, wait a minute, what is all this?' Carmody asked as he followed the space-suited people through the forest.

'Who are you people? What are you doing here?'

'Criminy!' the girl said, flushing with embarrassment. 'We've been rushing around so, we haven't even introduced ourselves! A fine lot of fools you must take us for, Mr Carmody!'

'Not at all,' Carmody said courteously. 'But I would like to know – well, to *know*, if you know what I mean.'

'Of course, I know what you mean,' the girl said. 'I am Aviva Christiansen, and this is my father, Professor Lars Christiansen.'

'You can knock off that "Professor" stuff,' Christiansen said gruffly. 'Just call me Lars, or Chris, or anything else that comes to mind.'

'All right, Dad,' Aviva said, with a mock show of fond petulance. 'Anyhow, Mr Carmody –'

'The name's Tom.'

'Tom, then,' Aviva said, colouring prettily. 'Where was I? Oh yes, Dad and I are connected with the Terran Interstellar Rescue Association (TIRA), which has its offices in Stockholm, Geneva, and Washington, DC.'

'I'm afraid I've never heard of your organization,' Carmody said.

'There's nothing surprising about that,' Aviva said. 'Earth has just entered upon the threshold of interstellar exploration. Even now, in laboratories all over the earth, new sources of power far exceeding the crude atomic devices to which you have been accustomed are now in the experimental stage. And very soon indeed, spacecraft piloted by men of Earth will probe to the farthest corners of the galaxy. And this will, of course, usher in a new period of international peace and cooperation upon our tired old planet.'

'It will?' Carmody asked. 'Why?'

'Because there will no longer be anything significant to fight about,' Aviva said, somewhat breathlessly since all three were trotting through low underbrush. 'There are countless worlds out there, as you may have noticed,' she continued, 'and there is room for all kinds of social experiments, and adventures, and everything you could possibly imagine. So man's energies will be directed outward instead of dissipated inward in the form of disastrous internecine warfare.'

'The kid's giving you the straight dope,' said Lars Christiansen, in his deep, gruff, friendly, no-nonsense voice. 'She may sound like a scatterbrain, but she's got about eleventy-seven Ph.Ds and Doctorates to back up her line of gab.'

'And my pop may sound like a roughneck,' Aviva flashed back, 'but he's got three Nobel prizes in his footlocker!'

Father and daughter exchanged looks which were somehow threatening and affectionate at the same time.

'So anyhow,' Aviva said, 'that's how it is, or I should say, how it's *going to be* in a couple of years. But we got a head start on it all due to Dr Maddox, whom you will meet shortly.' Aviva hesitated a moment, then said in a lower voice, 'I don't think I'll be betraying a confidence if I tell you that Dr Maddox is a – a – mutant.'

'Rats, there's no need to be nervous about the word,' Lars Christiansen growled. 'A mutant can be every bit as good as we are. And in the case of Dr Maddox, he can be about a thousand times better!'

'It was Dr Maddox who really put this project into orbit,' Aviva went on. 'You see, he made a projection of the future (how he does it I don't know!) and he realized that soon, with the imminent discovery of cheap, unlimited power in a safe, portable form, there were going to be spaceships all over the place! And a lot of people would just rush into space without proper equipment or navigational instruments or stuff –'

'A lot of half-baked fools,' Christiansen commented drily.

'Dad! Anyhow, these people were going to need help. But there would be no organized Galactic Rescue Patrol (he computed this figure very carefully) for 87·238874 years. Do you see?'

'I think so,' Carmody said. 'You three saw the problem and – and you stepped in.'

'Yes,' she said simply. 'We stepped in. Dad's very keen on serving others, though you could never tell it from the grouchy way he talks. And what's good enough for my dad is good enough for me. And as for Dr Maddox – well, he's just the utter maximum top realized-potential of any human being of my acquaintance.'

'Yeah, he's that all right, in spades, doubled,' Lars Christiansen said quietly. 'The man has had quite a history. Mutations are usually of negative value, you know. Just one or two out of a thousand pan out gold instead of pyrites. But in Dr Maddox's case, there is a family history of massive mutation, most of it favourable, all of it inexplicable.'

'We suspect benevolent alien intervention,' Aviva said, almost in a whisper. 'The Maddox family can only be traced back for two hundred years. It's a strange story. Aelill Madoxxe, Maddox's great-grandfather, was a Welsh coal miner. He worked for nearly twenty years in the notorious Auld Gringie Mine, and was one of the few labourers to retain his health. That was in 1739. Recently, when Auld Gringie was reopened, the fabulous Scatter-wail uranium deposits were found adjacent to it.'

'It must have begun there,' Christiansen said. 'We pick up the family next in 1801, in Oaxaca, Mexico. Thomas Madoxxe (as he styled himself) had married the beautiful and imperious Teresita de Valdez, Contessa de Aragon, owner of the finest hacienda in southern Mexico. Thomas was out riding herd on the morning of April 6th, 1801, when La Estrella Roja de Muerto – Red Star of Death (subsequently identified as a large, highly radioactive meteorite) – fell within two miles of the ranch. Thomas and Teresita were among the few survivors.'

'Next we come to the 1930s,' Aviva said, picking up the tale. 'The next Maddox generation, much reduced in wealth, moved to Los Angeles. Ernest Maddox, the doctor's grandfather, was selling a new-fangled contraption to doctors and dentists. It was called an "X-ray machine." Maddox demonstrated the machine twice weekly for at least ten years. He used himself as subject. Despite the massive overdose of hard radiation, *or perhaps because of it*, he lived to a very respectable age.'

'His son,' Lars said, 'moved by we know not what compulsion, travelled to Japan in 1935 and became a Zen monk. He lived in a *tsuktsuri,* or corner of an abandoned basement, throughout the war years, never once uttering a word. The local people left him alone, thinking he was an eccentric Pakistani. Maddox's basement was in Hiroshima, just 7.9 miles from the epicentre of the atomic explosion of 1945. *Immediately after the explosion,* Maddox left Japan and went to the Hui-Shen monastery, situated on the most inaccessible peak in northern Tibet. According to the story of an English tourist who was there at the time, *the lamas had been expecting him!* He settled there, devoting himself to the study of certain Tantras. He married a woman of royal Kashmiri blood, by whom he had one son: that was Owen, our doctor. The family left Tibet for the United States one week before the Red Chinese launched their invasion. Owen was educated at Harvard, Yale, UCLA, Oxford, Cambridge, the Sorbonne, and Heidelberg. How he found us is quite a strange story in itself, which you shall hear upon a more propitious occasion. For now we have reached the ship, and I think we dare not waste any more time in palaver.'

Carmody saw it in a little clearing, a majestic spaceship which rose upwards like a skyscraper. It possessed vanes, jets, hatches, and many other protuberances. In front of it, seated in a folding chair, was a man somewhat above middle age, with a benevolent, deeply creased face. It was immediately apparent that this man was Maddox the Mutant, for he had seven fingers on each hand, and his forehead bulged hugely to make room for the extra brain behind it.

Maddox rose in a leisurely manner (on five legs!) and nodded in welcome. 'You have come only just in time,' he said. 'Lines of inimical force have very nearly reached the intersection point. Come into the ship quickly, all of you! We must erect the force-shield without delay.'

Lars Christiansen marched forward, too proud to run. Aviva took Carmody's arm, and Carmody perceived that she was trembling, and that the shapeless grey cloth of her suit could not conceal the lissome lines of the beautiful girl, though she seemed unaware of it.

'It's a nasty situation,' Maddox muttered, folding his canvas chair and putting it within the ship. 'My calculations allow for this sort of nodal point, of course, but by the very nature of interminable combination one cannot predict their configuration. Still, we do our best.'

At the wide entrance hatch, Carmody hesitated. 'I really think I should say goodbye to Mr Maudsley,' he told Maddox. 'Perhaps I should even ask his advice. He's been very helpful, and he's working on a way to get me back to Earth.'

'Maudsley!' Maddox cried, exchanging significant glances with Christiansen. 'I suspected he was behind this!'

'It looked like his damned handiwork,' Christiansen grated.

'What do you mean?' Carmody asked.

'I mean,' Maddox said, 'that you have been victim and pawn in a vast conspiracy involving no fewer than seventeen star-systems. I cannot explain it all now; but believe me, not only your life and ours is at stake, but also the life of several dozen billion humanoids, most of them blue-eyed and fair-skinned!'

'Oh Tom, hurry, hurry!' Aviva cried, pulling at his arm.

'Well, all right,' Carmody said. 'But I shall want a complete and satisfactory explanation.'

'And you shall have it,' Maddox said as Carmody stepped through the hatch. 'You shall have it right now.'

Carmody turned quickly, detecting the note of menace in Maddox's voice. He looked at the mutant intently and experienced a wave of shock. He looked again, at his three rescuers, and really saw them for the first time.

The human mind is adept at constructing gestalts. A few curves suffice for a mountain, and half a dozen broken lines can produce a passable wave. The gestalt was breaking down now under Carmody's particularizing gaze. He saw that Aviva's lovely eyes were stylized and suggestive rather than functional – like the design of eyes on the wings of a moth. Lars had a dark red oval in the lower third of his face, divided by a darker line; this was supposed to be a mouth. Maddox's fingers, all seven of them, were painted on his body at thigh level.

The gestalt broke down completely. Carmody saw the thin black line, like a crack in the floor, that connected each of them to the ship. He stood, frozen, and watched them move towards him. They had no hands to raise, no feet to move, no eyes to see with, no mouth to explain with. They were in fact round-topped and featureless cylinders, artfully but superficially disguised as human. They had no parts with which to function; they were themselves parts, and they were now performing their sole function. They were the exact and terrible counterpart of three fingers on a giant's hand. They advanced with supple bonelessness; they evidently wanted to drive him deeper into the black maw of the ship.

The ship? Carmody darted around the three and raced back the way he had come in. But the hatch extruded pointed teeth from top and bottom, opened a little wider, and then began to close. How could he have thought it was metal? The dark shiny sides of the ship rippled now and began to contract. His feet were caught in the spongy, sticky deck, and the three fingers were moving around him, blocking him off from the diminishing square of daylight.

Carmody struggled with the desperation of a fly caught in a spider's web (the simile was exact, but the insight had come too late). He fought with a frenzy and with no effect. The square of daylight had become round and wet, and shrunk to the size of a baseball. The three cylinders were holding him now, and Carmody could not tell one from the other.

That was the final horror; that, and the fact that the walls and ceiling of the spaceship (or whatever it was) had turned a moist and livid red, and were closing in and engulfing him.

There was no escape. Carmody was helpless, unable to move or shout, unable to do anything but lose consciousness.

Chapter 16

As from a vast distance, Carmody heard a voice say: 'What do you think, Doctor? Can you do anything for him?'

He recognized that voice; it was the Prize.

'I'll pay for it,' another voice said. He recognized this as Maudsley. 'Do you think you can do anything for him?'

'He can be saved,' said a third voice, presumably that of the doctor. 'Medical science admits no limits to the feasible, only to the tolerable, which is the patient's limitation, not ours.'

Carmody struggled to open his eyes or his mouth, but found that he was completely immobilized.

'So it's serious, huh?' asked the Prize.

'That is a difficult question to answer with precision,' the doctor said. 'To begin with, we must assign categories. Medical science is easier than medical ethics, for example. We of the Galactic Medical Association are supposed to preserve life; we are also supposed to act in the best interests of the particular form we treat. But what should we do when these two imperatives are in contradiction? The Uiichi of Devin V, for example, seek a physician's aid to cure them of life and help them achieve their desired goal of death. It is a damnably difficult task, let me say, and only possible when an Uiichi has grown old and enfeebled. But what does ethics have to say about this strange reversal of normal desire? Are we to do as the Uiichi desire, and perform acts which are reprehensible in nearly every corner of the galaxy? Or are we to act upon the basis of our own standards, and thus doom the Uiichi to a fate quite literally worse than death?'

'What has this got to do with Carmody?' Maudsley asked.

'Not very much,' the doctor admitted. 'But I thought you might find it interesting, and it will help you see why we must charge the high fees we do.'

'Is he in a serious condition?' the Prize demanded.

'Only the dead can be said to be in a really serious condition,' the doctor stated. 'And even then, there are exceptions. Pentathanaluna, for example, which laymen refer to as Five-Day Reversible Death, is really no worse than a common cold, despite vulgar rumours to the contrary.'

'But what about Carmody?' Maudsley asked.

'He is definitely not dead,' the doctor said soothingly. 'He is merely in a state of – or tantamount to – deep shock. To put it more simply, he has, in a manner of speaking, fainted.'

'Can you pull him out of it?' the Prize asked.

'Your terms are unclear,' the doctor said. 'My work is difficult enough without –'

'I mean, can you restore him to his original state of function?' the Prize asked.

'Well! That is rather a large order, as I think you will admit if you give it a moment's thought. What *was* his original state of function? Does either of you know? Would he know himself if, miraculously, he could be consulted in his own cure? Of the million subtle alterations of personality, some of which take place at the mere instigation of a heartbeat, how can we know which was most characteristically *his*? Is not a lost personality like a lost second – something we can approximate but never truly reproduce? These, gentlemen, are questions of some weight.'

'Damnably heavy,' Maudsley said. 'Suppose you just get him as near to what he was as you can. Will that be very tough?'

'Not on me,' the doctor said. 'I have worked for a considerable time in my profession. I have become inured to the most ghastly sights, accustomed to the most hideous procedures. That is not to say that I have grown *callous*, of course; I have merely learned through sad necessity to direct my attention away from the soul-searing procedures which my profession demands of me.'

'Cripes, Doc!' the Prize said. 'What do you gotta do to my buddy?'

'I must operate,' the doctor said. 'It is the only reliable way. I shall dissect Carmody (speaking in layman's terms) and put his limbs and organs into a preserving solution. Then, I shall soften him in a dilute solution of K-5. I will draw his brain and nervous system out through various orifices. The procedure then is to hook up the nervous system and brain to a Life-Simulator, and fire the synapses in carefully timed series. Thus we see if there are any breaks, bad valves, stoppages, and the like. Assuming the absence of these, we disassemble the brain, coming at last to the interaction point between mind and body. Removing this very carefully, we check all internal and external connections. If everything is all right up to this point, we open the interaction-point reservoir, looking for leaks, of course, and then checking the level of consciousness within. If it is low of depleted (and in cases like these, it almost always is) we analyse the residue and create a new batch. This new batch of consciousness is tested exhaustively, then injected into the interaction-point reservoir. All parts of the corpus are then reassembled, and the patient can be reanimated with the Life-Simulator. That's pretty much the whole process.'

'Hooee,' said the Prize. 'I wouldn't treat a dog that way!'

'Nor would I,' the doctor said. 'Not until the canine race has evolved further. Do you wish me to perform this operation?'

'Well . . .' the Prize mused. 'I guess we can't just leave him lying around unconscious, can we?'

'Of course we can't,' Maudsley said. 'The poor fellow has been counting on us and we must not fail him. Doctor, do your duty!'

Carmody had been struggling with his malfunction-ing functions through this entire conversation. He had listened with steadily mounting terror and with the grow-ing conviction that his friends could do him more harm than his enemies could even imagine. Now, with a titanic effort, he burst open his eyes and wrenched his tongue away from the roof of his mouth.

'No operation!' he croaked. 'I'll cut your goddamned heart out if you try any goddamned operation!'

'He has recovered his faculties,' the doctor said, sound-ing quite pleased. 'Often, you know, a verbalization of our operating procedure in the patient's presence serves as a better anodyne than the operation itself. It is a placebo effect, of course, but certainly not to be sneered at.'

Carmody struggled to stand up, and Maudsley helped him to his feet. He looked at the doctor for the first time, and saw a tall, thin, mournful man in black clothes, who looked exactly like Abraham Lincoln. The Prize was no longer a cauldron. Evidently under the stress, he had changed into a dwarf.

'Send for me if you need me,' the doctor said, and de-parted.

'What happened?' Carmody asked. 'That spaceship, those people – '

'We pulled you out just in time,' the Prize said. 'But that was no spaceship, keed.'

'I know. What was it?'

'That,' Maudsley said, 'was your predator. You walked right into his mouth.'

'I guess I did at that,' Carmody said.

'And by doing that, you may have lost your only chance

of getting back to Earth,' Maudsley said. 'I think you'd better sit down, Carmody. You have only a few choices now, and none of them is particularly enticing.'

Carmody sat down.

Chapter 17

First and foremost, Maudsley talked about predators, their folkways and mores, habits and reactions, ways and means. It was important for Carmody to know just what had happened to him, and why, even if that knowledge came subsequent to the event.

'*Especially* if it comes after the event,' the Prize put in.

Maudsley went on to say that, just as for every man there's a woman, so for every living organism there's a predator. The Great Chain of Eating (a poetic image for the totality of life in a state of dynamism in the Universe) must go on, for reasons of inner necessity if for nothing else. Life as we know it involves creation; and creation is inconceivable without death. Thus –

'Why is creation inconceivable without death?' Carmody asked.

'Don't ask stupid questions. Where was I? Oh, yes. Thus murder is justified, though some of its concomitants are less readily appreciated. A creature in its natural habitat lives off certain other creatures and is lived off by still other creatures. This process is usually so natural and simple, and in so fine a state of balance, that preyers and preyed-upon alike tend to ignore it for great stretches of time, putting their attention instead upon the creation of art objects, the gathering of groundnuts, the contemplation of the Absolute, or whatever else the species finds of interest. And that is as it should be, because Nature (whom we may personify as an old lady dressed in russet and black) does not like to find her rules and regulations the subject of every cocktail party, swarming nest, Konklave, or what you will. But you, Carmody, by inadvertently escaping the checks and balances of your native planet, still have not escaped the inexorable Law of Process. Thus, if there were no existing predator for you in the farflung reaches of space, then one would have to be found. If one could not be found, then it would have to be created.'

'Well, yeah,' Carmody said. 'But that spaceship, those people –'

' – were not what they seemed,' Maudsley told him. 'That must be evident to you.'

'It is now.'

'*They* were actually *it*, a single entity, a creature created especially for you, Carmody. *It* was your predator, and it followed almost classically the simple, standard Laws of Predation.'

'Which are?' Carmody asked.

'Yes, which are,' the Prize sighed. 'How nicely you put it! We may rant against fortune and the world, but we are left at the end with the stark proposition: *These are the things which are.*'

'I wasn't commenting,' Carmody said, 'I was asking. What are these Laws of Predation?'

'Oh, sorry, I misunderstood you,' the Prize said.

'That's quite all right,' Carmody said.

'Thank you,' the Prize said,

'It's nothing,' Carmody said. 'I didn't mean . . . No, I did mean! What are these simple, standard Laws of Predation?'

'Must you ask?' Maudsley said.

'Yes, I'm afraid I must.'

'When you put it in the form of a question,' Maudsley said severely, 'predation ceases to be simple and standard, and even its status as a law becomes dubious. Knowledge of predation is inherent in all organisms, just like arms and legs and heads, but even more certain. It is much more basic than a law of science, you see, and therefore not subject to simplistic reductionism. The mere asking of that sort of question imposes a severe restriction upon the answer.'

'Still, I think I should know everything possible about predation,' Carmody said. 'Particularly mine.'

'Yes, definitely you should know,' Maudsley said. 'Or rather, you *should have known,* which is by no means the same thing. Still, I'll try.'

Maudsley rubbed his forehead vigorously and stated: 'You eat, therefore you are eaten. That much you know. But *how,* precisely, are you to be eaten? How are you to be trapped, seized, immobilized, and prepared? Will you be served up piping hot or nicely chilled or at room temperature? Obviously, that depends on the tastes of that which feasts upon you. Shall your predator leap at your undefended back from a convenient height? Shall it dig a pit for you, or spin a web, or challenge you to single combat, or dive upon you with outstretched talons? That depends upon your predator's nature, which determines his form and function. That nature is limited by and respondent to the exigencies of your own nature, which, like his, is informed by free will and thus ultimately unfathomable.

'Now to particulars. Diving, digging or spinning are straightforward, but they lose effectiveness against a creature with the faculty of memory. A creature like youself, Carmody, could you avoid the simplistic deadly attack once, might never be deceived again.

'Straightforwardness is not Nature's way, however. It has been said that Nature has a vested interest in illusions, which are highways to death and birth. I for one will not argue the proposition. If we accept the concept, we see that your predator must engage in complex manoeuvres in order to snare a complex creature such as yourself.

'There is another side to the problem also. Your predator was not conceived solely in order to eat you. You are the single most important thing in his life, granted; but he does possess free will, just as you do, and therefore is not limited to the strict logic of his eating function. Barn mice may think that the owl in the rafters was conceived and delineated for the sole purpose of hunting mice. But we know that the owl has several other things on his mind. This is how it is with all predators, including yours. From this, we draw an important conclusion: that all predators are functionally imperfect by virtue of their free will.'

'I never thought of it that way before,' Carmody said. 'Does that help me?'

'Well, not really. But I thought you should know it anyhow. You see, practically speaking, you may never be able to exploit your predator's imperfections. Indeed, you may never even learn what they are. In this situation you are just like the barn mice. You may find a hole to scamper in when you hear the whirr of wings, but you will never be able to analyse the nature, talents, and limitations of the owl.'

'Well, that's just great,' Carmody said, with heavy sarcasm. 'I'm licked before I start. Or, to use your terminology, I'm as good as eaten even though nobody's stuck a fork in me yet.'

'Temper, temper,' the Prize cautioned. 'It isn't quite as bad as that.'

'So how bad is it? Can either of you tell me anything useful?'

'That's what we're trying to do,' Maudsley said.

'Then tell me what this predator looks like.'

Maudsley shook his head. 'That is quite impossible. Do you think any victim can learn what his predator looks like? If he could, the victim would become immortal!'

'And that's against the rules,' the Prize put in.

'At least give me an idea,' Carmody said. 'Does he always go around disguised as a spaceship?'

'Of course not,' Maudsley said. 'From your point of view, he is a shape-changer. Have you ever heard of a mouse walking into the jaws of a snake, or a fly lighting on a frog's tongue, or a fawn stepping between the forepaws of a tiger? *That* is the essence of predation! And you must ask yourself: where did those deluded victims think they were going, and what did they think was in front of them? Similarly, you must ask yourself what was really in front of your eyes when you talked to three of the predator's fingers and followed them straight into his mouth!'

'They looked like people,' Carmody said. 'But I still don't know what the predator looked like.'

'There is no way I can enlighten you,' Maudsley said. 'Information about predators is not easily gained. They are too complementary to oneself. Its traps and concealments are based upon your own memories, your dreams and fantasies, your hopes and desires. The predator takes your own treasured dramas and plays them for you, as you just saw. To know your predator, you must know yourself. And it is easier to know the entire Universe than to know oneself.'

'What can I do?' Carmody asked.

'Learn!' Maudsley said. 'Be eternally vigilant, move at top speed, trust nothing and no one. Don't think of relaxing until you have reached your home.'

'Home!' Carmody said.

'Yes. You will be safe on your own planet. Your predator cannot enter your lair. You will still be subject to all commonplace disasters, but at least you will be spared this.'

'Can you send me home?' Carmody asked. 'You said you were working on a machine.'

'I have completed it,' Maudsley said. 'But you must understand its limitations, which are a concomitant with my own. My machine can take you to Where Earth is now, but that is all it can do.'

'But that's all I need!' Carmody said.

'No, it is not. "Where" gives you only the first W of location. You will still have to solve for When and Which.

Take them in order, is my advice. Temporality before particularity, to use a common expression. You will have to leave here at once; your predator, whose appetite you foolishly aroused, may be back at any instant. I may not be so lucky this time in my rescue attempts.'

'How did you get me out of his mouth?' Carmody asked.

'I hastily fabricated a lure,' Maudsley told him. 'It looked just like you, but I built it a little larger than life-size and gave it a bit more vitality. The predator dropped you and bounded after it, dribbling saliva. But we can't try that again.'

Carmody preferred not to ask if the lure had felt any pain. 'I'm ready,' he said. 'But where am I going, and what is going to happen?'

'You are going to an Earth, almost undoubtedly the wrong one. But I will send a letter to a person I know who is very clever at solving temporal problems. He'll look you up, if he decides to take your case, and after that . . . well, who can say? Take it as it comes, Carmody, and be grateful if anything comes at all.'

'I am grateful,' Carmody said. 'No matter what the outcome, I want to thank you very much.'

'That's quite all right,' Maudsley said. 'Don't forget my message to the old fellow if you ever do get back home. All set to go? The machine is right here beside me. I didn't have time to make it visible, but it looks almost exactly like a Zenith battery-operated shortwave radio. Where the hell did it go? Here it is. Got your Prize?'

'I've got him,' the Prize said, holding on to Carmody's left arm with both hands.

'Then we're ready. I set this dial here and then this one, and then these two over here . . . You'll find it pleasant to be out of the macrocosm, Carmody, and back on a planet, even if it isn't yours. There's no qualitative difference, of course, among atom, planet, galaxy or universe. It's all a question of what scale you live on most comfortably. And now I push *this* –'

Bam! Pow! Crrrrunch! Slow dissolve, quick dissolve, lap dissolve, electronic music denoting outer space, outer space denoting electronic music. Pages of a calendar flip, Carmody tumbles head over heels in simulated free fall. Kettledrums sound ominous note, ominous note sounds kettledrums, bright flash of colours, woman's voice keening in echo chamber, laughter of children, montage of Jaffa oranges lighted to look like planets, collage of a solar system lighted to look like ripples in a brook. Slow the tape, speed the tape, fade out, fade in.

It was one hell of a trip, but nothing Carmody hadn't expected.

Part Three

When is Earth?

Chapter 18

With the transition completed, Carmody took stock of himself. A brief inventory convinced him that he still had all four limbs, one body, one head, and one mind. Final returns were not in, of course, but he did seem to be all there. He also noted that he still had the Prize, which was somehow recognizable even though it had undergone its usual metamorphosis. This time it had changed from a dwarf into a badly constructed flute.

'So far, so good,' Carmody said to nobody in particular. He now surveyed his surroundings.

'Not so good,' he said at once. He had been prepared to arrive at the wrong Earth, but he hadn't expected it would be quite so wrong as this.

He was standing on marshy ground at the edge of a swamp. Miasmic vapours rose from the stagnant brown waters. There were broad-leaved ferns, and low, thin-leaved shrubs, and bushy-headed palms, and a single dogwood tree. The air was blood-warm and heavily laden with odours of fertility and decay.

'Maybe I'm in Florida,' Carmody said hopefully.

'Afraid not,' said the Prize, or the flute, speaking in a low melodious voice but with an excess of vibrato.

Carmody glared at the Prize. 'How come you can speak?' he demanded.

'How come you didn't ask me that when I was a cauldron?' the Prize replied. 'But I'll tell you, if you really want to know. Affixed up here, just inside my mouth-piece, is a CO_2 cartridge. That serves me in place of lungs, though for a limited time only. The rest is obvious.'

It wasn't obvious to Carmody. But he had more important matters on his mind. He asked, 'Where am I?'

'*We*,' said the Prize, 'are on the planet Earth. This moist bit of ground upon which we are standing will become, in your day, the township of Scarsdale, New York.' He snickered. 'I suggest you buy property now, while the real-estate values are depressed. '

'It sure as hell doesn't look like Scarsdale,' Carmody said.

'Of course not. Leaving aside for a moment the question of *Whichness,* we can see that the *Whenness* is all wrong.'

'Well . . . *When* are we?'

'A good question,' the Prize replied, 'but one to which I can only make an approximate and highly qualified reply. Obviously enough, we are in the Phanerozoic Aeon, which in itself covers one sixth of Earth's geological time. Easy enough; but what *part* of the Phanerozoic are we in, the Palaeozoic or the Mesozoic Era? Here I must hazard a guess. Just on the basis of climate, I rule out all of the Palaeozoic except, just possibly, the end of the Permian Period. But wait, now I can rule that out, too! Look, overhead and to your right!'

Carmody looked and saw an oddly shaped bird flapping awkwardly into the distance.

'Definitely an Archaeopteryx,' the Prize said. 'You could tell at once from the way its feathers diverged pinnately from its axis. Most scientists consider it a creature of the upper Jurassic and the Cretaceous Periods, but certainly not older than the Triassic. So we can rule out the entire Palaeozoic; we are definitely in the Mesozoic Era.'

'That's pretty far back, huh?' Carmody said.

'Quite far,' the Prize agreed. 'But we can do better than that. I think we can pinpoint what part of the Mesozoic we are in. Let me think for a bit.' He thought for a bit. 'Yes, I think I have it. *Not* the Triassic! That swamp is a false clue, I fear. However, the angiospermous flowering plant near your left foot points an unmistakable direction, periodwise. Nor does it constitute our sole evidence. You noticed the dogwood tree in front of you? Well, turn around and you will see two poplars and a fig tree in the midst of a small group of conifers. Significant, eh? But did you notice the most important detail of all, so commonplace in your time that you would be apt to overlook it? I refer to grass, which we see here in abundance. There was no grass as late as Jurassic times! Just ferns and cycadeoids! And that decides it, Carmody! I'd wager my life savings on it! We are in the Cretaceous Period, and probably not far from its upper limit!'

Carmody had only the vaguest remembrance of the geological periods of the Earth. 'Cretaceous,' he said. 'How far is that from my time?'

'Oh, about a hundred million years, give or take a few million,' the Prize said. 'The Cretaceous age lasted for seventy million years.'

Carmody had no difficulty in adjusting to this concept; he never even tried. He said to the Prize, 'How did you learn all of this geology stuff?'

'How do you think?' the Prize replied spiritedly. 'I studied. I figured, since we were going to Earth, I'd better find out something about the place. And it's a damned good thing I did. If it weren't for me, you'd be stumbling around here looking for Miami Beach, and you'd have probably ended up being eaten by an allosaurus.'

'Eaten by a who?'

'I refer,' the Prize said, 'to one of the uglier members of the order Saurischia, an offshoot of which – the sauropoda – culminated in the renowned brontosaurus.'

'You mean to tell me there are dinosaurs here?' Carmody asked.

'I mean to tell you,' the Prize said in obbligato, 'that this is the one and original Dinosaursville, and I would also like to take this opportunity to welcome you to the Age of the Giant Reptiles.'

Carmody made an incoherent noise. He noticed a movement to his left and turned. He saw a dinosaur. It looked about twenty feet high, and might have stretched fifty feet from nose to tail. It stood erect on its hind legs. It was coloured slate-blue, and it was striding rapidly towards Carmody.

'Is that a tyrannosaurus?' Carmody asked.

'Yes, it is,' the Prize said. '*Tyrannosaurus rex,* most highly respected of the saurischians. A true deinodon, you will note, its upper incisors running half a foot in length. This young chap coming towards us must weigh upwards of nine tons.'

'And he eats meat,' Carmody said.

'Yes, of course. I personally think that tyrannosaurus and other camosaurs of this period feasted mainly on the inoffensive and widely distributed hadrosaurs. But that is only my own pet theory.'

The giant creature was less than fifty feet away. There was no refuge on the flat, marshy land, no place to climb, no cave to scuttle into. Carmody said, 'What should I do?'

'You must change into a plant at once!' the Prize said urgently.

'But I can't!'

'You can't? Then your situation is serious indeed. Let me see, you can't fly or burrow, and I'd wager ten to one you'd never outrun him. Hmm, this becomes difficult.'

'So what do I do?'

'Well, under the circumstances, I think you should be stoical about the whole thing. I could quote Epictetus to you. And we could sing a hymn together if that would help.'

'Damn your hymns! I want to get out of this!'

The flute had already begun to play 'Nearer My God to Thee.' Carmody clenched his fists. The tyrannosaurus was now directly in front of him, towering overhead like a fleshed-out and animate derrick. It opened its awesome mouth.

Chapter 19

'Hello,' said the tyrannosaurus. 'My name is Emie and I am six years old. What's your name?'

'Carmody,' said Carmody.

'And I'm his Prize,' said the Prize.

'Well, you both look very strange,' said Emie. 'You don't look like anybody I've ever met before, and I've met a dimetrodon, and a struthiomimus, and a scolosaurus, and lots of others. Do you come from around here?'

'Well, sort of,' Carmody said. Then, reflecting on the dimensionality of time, he said, 'But not really, actually.'

'Oh,' said Emie. Childlike, he stared at them and fell into a silence. Carmody stared back, fascinated by that huge, grim head, larger than a slot machine or a beer keg, the narrow mouth studded with teeth like rows of stilettos. Fearsome indeed! Only the eyes – which were round, mild, blue and trusting – refuted the rest of the dinosaur's ominous appearance.

'Well, so,' Emie said at last, 'what are you doing here in the park?'

'Is this a park?' Carmody asked.

'Sure, it's a park!' Emie said. 'It's a park for *kids,* and I don't think you're a kid, even though you are very small.'

'You're right, I'm not a kid,' Carmody said. 'I stumbled into your park by mistake. I think perhaps I should speak to your father.'

'Hokay,' Emie said. 'Climb on my back and I'll take you to him. And don't forget, I discovered you. And bring along your friend. He's *really* strange!'

Carmody slipped the Prize into his pocket and mounted the tyrannosaurus, finding hand and foot holds on the folds of Emie's iron-tough skin. As soon as he was securely in place on the dinosaur's neck, Emie wheeled and began to lope towards the southwest.

'Where are we going?' Carmody asked.

'To see my father.'

'Yes, but where *is* your father?'

'He's in the city, working at his job. Where else would he be?'

'Of course, where else indeed?' Carmody said, taking a firmer grip as Emie broke into a gallop.

From Carmody's pocket, the Prize said, in a muffled voice, 'This is all exceedingly strange.'

'You're the strange one around here,' Carmody reminded him. Then he settled back to enjoy the ride.

They didn't call it Dinosaursville, but Carmody could think of it in no other way. It lay about two miles from the park. First they came to a road, a wide trail, actually, stamped to the firmness of concrete, by countless dinosaur feet. They followed it and passed many hadrosaurs sleeping beneath willow trees by the side of the road and occasionally harmonizing in low, sweet voices. Carmody asked about them, but Emie would only say that his father considered them a real problem.

The road went past groves of birch, maple, laurel and holly. Each grove had its dozen or so dinosaurs, moving purposefully beneath the branches, digging at the ground or pushing away refuse. Carmody asked what they were doing.

'They're tidying up,' Emie said scornfully. 'That's all that housewives ever do.'

They had come to an upland plateau. They left the last individual grove behind and plunged abruptly into a forest.

Evidently it was not a natural growth; it showed many signs of having been planted purposefully and with considerable foresight. Its outer trees consisted of a broad belt of fig, breadfruit, hazelnut and walnut. Past that there were several nicely spaced rows of tall, slim-trunked gingkos. Then, there was nothing but pine trees and an occasional spruce.

As they moved deeper into the forest, it became more and more crowded with dinosaurs. Most of these were theropods – carnivorous tyrannosaurs like Emie. But the Prize also pointed out several ornithopods, and literally hundreds of the ceratopsia offshoot represented by the massively horned triceratops. Nearly all of them moved through the trees at a canter. The ground shook beneath their feet, the trees trembled, and clouds of dust were flung into the air. Flank scraped against armoured flank, collisions were avoided only by quick turns, abrupt halts and sudden accelerations. There was much bellowing for right-of-way. The sight of several thousand hurrying dinosaurs was almost as fearsome as their smell, which was overpowering.

'Here we are,' said Emie, stopping so quickly that Carmody was nearly thrown off his neck. 'This is my dad's place!'

Carmody looked around and saw that Emie had brought him to a small grove of sequoias. The big trees formed an oasis within the forest. Two or three dinosaurs moved among the redwoods with a slow, almost languid pace, ignoring the turmoil fifty yards away. Carmody decided that he could get down without being trampled upon. Warily he slid off Emie's neck.

'Dad!' Emie shouted. 'Hey, Dad, just look what I found, look, Dad!'

One of the dinosaurs looked up. He was a tyrannosaur, somewhat larger than Emie, with white striations across his blue hide. His eyes were grey and bloodshot. He turned around with great deliberation.

'How often,' he asked, 'have I asked you not to gallop here?'

'I'm sorry, Dad, but look, I found –'

'You are always "sorry,"' the tyrannosaur said, 'but you never see fit to modify your behaviour. I have spoken with your mother about this, Emie, and we are in substantial agreement. Neither of us wishes to raise a graceless, loud-mouthed hot-rodder who doesn't possess the manners of a brontosaurus. I love you, my son, but you must learn –'

'Dad! Will you please save the lecture for later and look, just *look*, at what I've found!'

The elderly tyrannosaur's mouth tightened and his tail flicked ominously. But he lowered his head, following the direction of his son's outstretched forepaw, and saw Carmody.

'Well bless my soul!' he cried.

'Good day, sir,' Carmody said. 'My name is Thomas Carmody. I am a human being. I don't think there are any other humans on Earth just now, or even any primates. How I got here is a little difficult to explain, but I come in peace, and – and that sort of thing,' he finished lamely.

'Fantastic!' Emie's father said. He turned his head. 'Baxley! Do you see what I see? Do you hear what I hear?'

Baxley was a tyrannosaur of about the same age as Emie's father. He said, 'I see it, Borg, but I don't believe it.'

'A talking mammal!' Borg exclaimed.

'I still don't believe it,' said Baxley.

Chapter 20

It took Borg longer to accept the idea of a talking mammal than it took Carmody to accept the idea of a talking reptile. Still, Borg finally did accept it. As the Prize remarked later, there is nothing like the actual presence of a fact to make one believe in the existence of that fact.

They retired to Borg's office, which was under the lofty green foliage of a weeping-willow tree. There, they sat and cleared their throats, trying to think of something to say. At last Borg said, 'So you're an alien mammal from the future, eh?'

'I guess I am,' Carmody said. 'And you are an indigenous reptile from the past.'

'I never thought about it that way,' Borg said. 'But yes, I suppose that's true. How far ahead in the future did you say you came from?'

'About a hundred million years or so.'

'Hah. Quite a long time away. Yes, a long time indeed.'

'It *is* quite a long time away,' Carmody agreed.

Borg nodded and hummed tunelessly. It was evident to Carmody that he didn't know what to say next. Borg seemed a very decent sort of person; hospitable, but set in his ways, very much a family man, no conversational-ist, just a decent, dull, middle-class tyrannosaur.

'Well, well,' Borg said, after the silence had become uncomfortable, 'and how *is* the future?'

'Beg pardon?'

'I mean, what sort of a place is the future?'

'Very busy,' Carmody replied. 'Bustling. Many new in-ventions, a great deal of confusion.'

'Well, well, well,' Borg said. 'That's very much as some of our more imaginative chaps had pictured it. Some of them have even predicted an evolutionary change in the mammals, making them the dominant species on Earth. But I consider that farfetched and grotesque.'

'I suppose it must sound that way,' Carmody said.

'Then you *are* the dominant species?'

'Well . . . *one* of the dominant species.'

'But what about the reptiles? Or more specifically, how are the tyrannosaurs doing in the future?'

Carmody had neither the heart nor the nerve to tell him that dinosaurs were extinct in his day, and had been extinct for sixty million years or so, and that reptiles in general had come to occupy an insignificant part in the scheme of things.

'Your race is doing every bit as well as could be ex-pected,' Carmody replied, feeling positively Pythian and rather sneaky.

'Good! I thought it would be like that!' Borg said. 'We're a tough race, you know, and most of us have will-power and common sense. Do men and reptiles have much trouble co-existing?'

'No, not much trouble,' Carmody said.

'Glad to hear it. I was afraid the dinosaurs might have become high-handed on account of their size.'

'No, no,' Carmody said. 'Speaking for the mammals of the future, I think I can safely say that everybody likes a dinosaur.'

'It's very decent of you to say that,' Borg said.

Carmody mumbled something. He suddenly felt very ashamed of himself.

'The future holds no great anxiety for a dinosaur,' Borg said, falling into the rotund tones of an after-dinner speaker. 'But it was not always that way. Our extinct ancestor, the allosaurus, seems to have been a bad-tempered brute and a gluttonous feeder. His ancestor, the ceratosaurus, was a dwarf carnosaur. To judge from the size of his braincase, he must have been incredibly stupid. There were other dawn-age carnosaurs, of course; and before them there must have been a missing link – a remote ancestor from which both the quadruped and the bipedal dinosaurs sprang.'

'The bipedal dinosaurs are dominant, of course?' Carmody asked.

'Of course. The triceratops is a dull-witted creature with a savage disposition. We keep small herds of them. Their flesh rounds out a meal of brontosaurus steak quite nicely. There are various other species, of course. You might have noticed some hadrosaurs as you came into the city.'

'Yes, I did,' Carmody said. 'They were singing.'

'Those fellows are always singing,' Borg said sternly.

'Do you eat them?'

'Good heavens, no! Hadrosaurs are *intelligent*! They are the only other intelligent species on the planet, aside from tyrannosaurs.'

'Your son said they were a real problem.'

'Well, they are,' Borg said, a little too defiantly.

'In what way?'

'They're lazy. Also sullen and surly. I know what I'm talking about; I've employed hadrosaurs as servants. They have no ambition, no drive, no stick-to-it-iveness. Half the time they don't know who hatched them, and they don't seem to care. They don't look you forthrightly in the eye when they speak to you.'

'They sing well, though,' Carmody said.

'Oh, yes, they sing well. Some of our best entertainers are hadrosaurs. They also do well at heavy construction, if given supervision. Their appearance works against them, of course, that duckbilled look ... But they can't help that. Has the hadrosaur problem been solved in the future?'

'It has,' Carmody said. 'The race is extinct.'

'Perhaps it's best that way,' Borg said. 'Yes, I really think it's best.'

Carmody and Borg conversed for several hours. Carmody learned about the problems of urban reptilian life. The forest-cities were becoming increasingly crowded as more and more tyrannosaurs and hadrosaurs left the country-side for the pleasures of civilization. A traffic problem of some severity had sprung up in the last fifty years. Giant saurischians like to travel fast and are proud of their quick reflexes. But when several thousand of them are rushing through a forest at the same time, accidents are bound to happen. The accidents were often severe: when two reptiles, each weighing forty tons, meet head-on at thirty miles an hour, broken necks are the most likely result.

These were not the only problems, of course. The overcrowded cities were a symptom of an exploding birthrate. Saurischians in various parts of the world lived on the edge of starvation. Disease and warfare tended to thin their numbers, but not enough.

'We have these and many other problems,' Borg said. 'Some of our finest minds have given way to despair. But I am more sanguine. We reptiles have seen difficult times before and have won through. We shall solve these problems just as we have solved all others. To my way of thinking, there is an innate nobility about our race, a spark of conscious, unquenchable life. I cannot believe that this will be extinguished.'

Carmody nodded and said, 'Your people will endure.' There really was nothing for him to do but lie like a gentleman.

'I know it,' Borg said. 'It is always good, however, to receive confirmation. Thank you for that. And now I suppose you would like to speak with your friends.'

'What friends?' Carmody asked.

'I refer to the mammal standing directly behind you,' Borg said.

Carmody turned quickly and saw a short, fat, bespectacled man in a dark business suit, with a briefcase and an umbrella under his left arm. 'Mr Carmody?' he asked.

'Yes, I'm Carmody,' Carmody said.

'I am Mr Surtees from the Bureau of Internal Revenue. You have given us quite a chase, Mr Carmody, but the IRS always gets its man.'

Borg said, 'This is none of my concern.' He exited, making very little noise for so large a tyrannosaurus.

'You have some unusual friends,' Mr Surtees said, gazing at the departing Borg. 'But that is no concern of mine, though it may be of some interest to the FBI. I am here solely in regard to your 1965 and 1966 tax returns. I have in my briefcase an extradition order, which I think you will find in order. My time machine is parked just outside of this tree. I suggest that you come along quietly.'

'No,' said Carmody.

'I beg you to reconsider,' said Surtees. 'The case against you can be settled to the mutual satisfaction of all concerned. But it must be settled at once. The government of the United States does not like to be kept waiting. Refusal to obey an order of the Supreme Court –'

'I told you, no!' Carmody said. 'You might as well go away. I know who you are.'

For this was the predator beyond any doubt. Its mimicry of an Internal Revenue man had been unbelievably clumsy. Both the briefcase and the umbrella were jointed to the left hand. The features were fair, but an ear had been forgotten. And, worst of all, the knees were hinged backwards.

Carmody turned and walked away. The predator stood there, not following, presumably unable to follow. It gave a single cry of hunger and rage. Then it disappeared.

Carmody had little time for self-congratulation, however, for a moment later, he disappeared.

Chapter 21

'Well, come in, come in.'

Carmody blinked. He was no longer exchanging views with a dinosaur in the Cretaceous age. Now he was somewhere else. He was in a small, dingy room. The floor was of stone, chilly to his feet. The windows were covered with soot. Tall candles trembled uneasily in the draught.

A man was seated behind a high rolltop desk. The man had a long nose jutting out of a long, bony face. His eyes were cavernous. There was a brown mole in the middle of his left cheek. His lips were thin and bloodless.

The man said, 'I am the Honourable Clyde Beedle Seethwright. And you are Mr Carmody, of course, whom Mr Maudsley so kindly referred to us. Do take that chair, sir. I trust that your trip from Mr Maudsley's planet was a pleasant one?'

'It was fine,' Carmody said, sitting down. He knew he was being ungracious, but the abrupt transitions were beginning to get him down.

'And Mr Maudsley is well?' Seethwright said, beaming.

'He's fine,' Carmody said. 'Where am I?'

'Didn't the clerk tell you on your way in?'

'I didn't see any clerk. I didn't even see myself come in.'

'My, my,' Seethwright said, and clucked mildly. 'The reception room must have gone out of phase again. I've had it fixed a dozen times, but it keeps on desynchronizing. It is vexing for my clients, and even worse for my poor clerk, who goes out of phase with it and sometimes can't get back to his family for a week or more.'

'That is a real tough break,' Carmody said, and found himself near hysteria. 'If you don't mind,' he said, keeping a tight control on his voice, 'just tell me what this place is and how I'm supposed to get home from here.'

'Calm yourself,' Mr Seethwright said. 'Perhaps a cup of tea? No? This "place," as you refer to it, is The Galactic Placement Bureau. Our articles of incorporation are on the wall, if you would care to read them.'

'How did I get here?' Carmody asked.

Mr Seethwright smiled and pressed his fingertips together. 'Very simply, sir. When I received Mr Maudsley's letter, I had a search made. The clerk found you on Earth B3444123C22. This was obviously the wrong place for you. I mean to say, Mr Maudsley had done his best, but he is *not* in the placement service. Therefore, I took the liberty of transporting you here. But if you wish to return to that aforementioned Earth –'

'No, no,' Carmody said. 'I was just wondering how . . . I mean, you said that this is a Galactic Placement Service, right?'

'*The* Galactic Placement Service,' Seethwright corrected gently.

'OK. So I'm not on Earth.'

'No indeed. Or, to put it more rigorously, you are not on any of the possible, probable, potential or temporal worlds of the Earth configuration.'

'OK, fine,' Carmody said. He was breathing heavily. 'Now, Mr Seethwright, have *you* ever been to any of those Earths?'

'I'm afraid I have never had the pleasure. My work keeps me pretty well tied to the office, you see, and I spend holidays at my family's cottage at –'

'Right!' Carmody thundered abruptly. 'You've never been to Earth, or so you claim! In that case, why in God's name are you sitting in a goddamned room like out of *Dickens* with *candles* yet and wearing a stove-pipe hat? Hey? Just let's hear you answer that one, because I already *know* the damned answer, which is that some son of a bitch must have *drugged* me and I dreamed this whole damned cockomamie thing including *you*, you grinning hatchet-faced bastard!'

Carmody collapsed in the chair, breathing like a steam engine and glaring triumphantly at Seethwright. He waited for everything to dissolve, for funny shapes to come and go, and for himself to wake up in his own bed in his own apartment, or maybe in a friend's bed or even in a hospital bed.

Nothing happened. Carmody's sense of triumph trickled away. He felt utterly confused, but he was suddenly too tired to care.

'Are you *quite* over your outburst?' Mr Seethwright asked frigidly.

'Yes, I'm over it,' Carmody said. 'I'm sorry.'

'Don't fret,' Seethwright said quietly. 'You have been under a strain; one appreciates that. But I can do nothing for you unless you keep control of yourself. Intelligence may lead you home; wild emotional outbursts will get you nowhere.'

'I really am sorry,' Carmody said.

'As for this room, which seems to have startled you so, I had it decorated especially for you. The period is only approximate – the best I could do on short notice. It was done to make you feel at home.'

'That was thoughtful of you,' Carmody said. 'I suppose that your appearance –'

'Yes, precisely,' Mr Seethwright said, smiling. 'I had myself decorated as well as the room. It was no trouble, really. It is the sort of little touch which so many of our clients appreciate.'

'I do appreciate it, as a matter of fact,' Carmody said. 'Now that I'm getting used to it, it's sort of restful.'

'I hoped you would find it soothing,' Seethwright said. 'As for your proposition that all of this is happening to you in a dream – well, it has some merit.'

'It has?'

Mr Seethwright nodded vigorously. 'It has definite merit as a proposition, but it has no validity as a statement of your circumstances.'

'Oh,' Carmody said, and sat back in the chair.

'Strictly speaking,' Seethwright went on, 'there is no important difference between imaginary and real events. The opposition you create between them is entirely verbal. You are not dreaming any of this, Mr Carmody; but I mention that only as a point of incidental information. Even if you were dreaming it all, you would have to pursue the same course of action.'

'I don't understand all that,' Carmody said. 'But I'll take your word that this is real.' He hesitated, then said, 'But the thing I *really* don't understand – why is all of this *like* this? I mean, the Galactic Centre looked a little like Radio City, and Borg the dinosaur didn't talk like any dinosaur, even a *talking* dinosaur, ought to talk, and –'

'Please, don't excite yourself,' Mr Seethwright said.

'Sorry,' Carmody said.

'You want me to tell you why reality is the way it is,' Seethwright said. 'But there is no explanation for that. You must simply learn to fit your preconceptions to what you find. You must not expect reality to adapt itself to you, except very infrequently. It can't be helped if things are strange; and it also can't be helped if things are familiar. Am I getting through?'

'I think so,' Carmody said.

'Splendid! You're sure you won't have some tea?'

'No, thank you.'

'Then we must see about getting you home,' Seethwright said. 'Nothing like the dear old place to pick up one's spirits, eh?'

'Nothing at all!' Carmody said. 'Will it be very difficult, Mr Seethwright?'

'No, I don't think I would characterize it as *difficult*,' Seethwright said. 'It will be complicated, of course, and rigorous, and even somewhat risky. But I do not consider any of those things to be *difficult*.'

'What *do* you consider truly difficult?' Carmody asked.

'Solving quadratic equations,' Seethwright answered at once. 'I simply cannot do them, even though I've tried a million or more times. That, sir, is a difficulty! Now let us proceed to your case.'

'Do you know where Earth is?' Carmody asked.

'"Where" poses no problem,' Seethwright said. 'You

have already been to Where, though it didn't do you much good, since When was so far off the mark. But now I think we can pin down your particular When without undue travail. It's the Which which gets tricky.'

'Is that likely to stop us?'

'Not at all,' Seethwright said. 'We must simply sort through and find which Which you belong in. The process is perfectly straightforward; like shooting fish in a barrel, as your people would say.'

'I've never tried that,' Carmody said. 'Is it really easy?'

'That depends upon the size of the fish and the size of the barrel,' Seethwright told him. 'It is, for example, nearly effortless to pot a shark in a bathtub; whereas it is a considerable undertaking to bring down a minnow in a hogshead. Scale is everything. But whichever project is before you, I think you can appreciate its essential straightforwardness and simplicity.'

'I suppose so,' Carmody said. 'But it occurs to me that my search for *Which* Earth may be straightforward and simple, but may also be impossible to complete due to the interminability of the series of selections.'

'That's not quite true but it's very nicely said,' Seethwright said, beaming. 'Complication is often very useful, you know. It helps to specify and identify the problem.'

'Well . . . What happens now?'

'Now we go to work,' Seethwright said, rubbing his hands together briskly. 'My staff and I have put together a selection of Which-worlds. We confidently expect that your world will be one of them. But of course, only you can determine the right one.'

'So I look them over and decide?' Carmody asked.

'Something like that,' Seethwright said. 'Actually, you must *live* them over. Then, as soon as you are sure, signify to us whether we've hit your probability-world or a variant. If it's your world, that's the end of it. If it's a variant, then we move you on to the next Which-world.'

'That sounds reasonable enough,' Carmody said. 'Are there a lot of these probability-worlds?'

'An interminable number, as you suspected earlier. But we have every hope of early success. Unless –'

'Unless what?'

'Unless your predator gets to you first.'

'My predator!'

'He is still on your trail,' Mr Seethwright said. 'And as you know by now, he is reasonably adept at setting snares. These snares take the form of scenes culled from your own memories. "Terraform scenes," I suppose we could call them, designed to lull and deceive you, to convince you to walk unsuspecting into his mouth.'

'Will he interfere with your worlds?' Carmody asked.

'Of course he will,' Seethwright said. 'There's no sanctuary in the searching process. On the contrary – the better and more informed the search, the more fraught it is with dangers. You had asked me earlier about dreams and reality. Well, here is your answer. Everything that helps you does so openly. Everything that seeks to harm you does so covertly, by the use of delusions, disguises, and dreams.'

'Isn't there anything you can do about the predator?' Carmody asked.

'Nothing. Nor would I if I could. Predation is a necessary circumstance. Even the Gods are eventually eaten by Fate. You will not be an exception to the universal rule.'

'I thought you'd say something like that,' Carmody said. 'But can you give me any help at all? Any hints on how the worlds you send me to will differ from the worlds of the predator?'

'To me the differences are obvious,' Seethwright said. 'But you and I do not share the same perceptions. You could not make use of my insights, Carmody; nor I of yours. Still, you have managed to elude the predator so far.'

'I've been lucky.'

'There you are! I have a great deal of skill, but no luck whatsoever. Who can tell which quality will be most needed in the trials ahead? Not I, sir, and certainly not you! Therefore be of stout heart, Mr Carmody. Faint heart ne'er won fair planet, eh? Look over the worlds I send you to, be extremely cautious of the predator's scenes of delusion, get out while the getting's good; but do not be unmanned by fear into passing up your true and rightful world.'

'What happens if I do pass it by inadvertently?' Carmody asked.

'Then your search can never end,' Seethwright told him. 'Only you can tell us where you belong. If, for one reason or another, you do not locate your world among the most likely, then we must continue our search among the merely likely, and then the less likely, and finally the least likely. The number of probability-worlds of Earth is not infinite, of course; but from your viewpoint, it might as well be; you simply do not have enough inherent duration to search through them all and then begin again.'

'All right,' Carmody said doubtfully. 'I don't suppose there's any other way.'

'There's no other way I can help you,' Seethwright said. 'And I doubt if there is any way at all that would not involve your active participation. But if you wish, I can make inquiries into alternative galactic location techniques. It would take a while –'

'I don't think I have a while,' Carmody said. 'I think my predator is not far behind me. Mr Seethwright, please send me to the probability-earths, and also accept my gratitude for your patience and interest.'

'Thank you,' Seethwright said, obviously pleased. 'Let us hope that the very first world will be the one you are seeking.'

Seethwright pressed a button on his desk. Nothing happened until Carmody blinked. Then things happened very quickly indeed, for Carmody unblinked and saw that he was smack dab on Earth. Or on a reasonable facsimile thereof.

Part Four

Which is Earth?

Chapter 22

Carmody was standing on a neatly trimmed plain, beneath a blue sky, with a golden-yellow sun overhead. He looked around slowly. Half a mile ahead of him he saw a small city. This city was not constructed in the common manner of an American city – with outliers of gas stations, tentacles of hot-dog stands, fringe of motels, and a protective shell of junkyards; but rather, as some Italian hill towns are fashioned, and some Swiss villages as well, suddenly rising and brusquely ending, without physical preamble or explanation, the main body of the town presenting itself all at once and without amelioration.

Despite its foreign look, Carmody felt sure that he was looking at an American city. So he advanced upon it, slowly and with heightened senses, prepared to flee if anything was amiss.

All seemed in order, however. The city had a warm and open look; its streets were laid out generously, and there was a frankness about the wide bay windows of its store fronts. As he penetrated deeper, Carmody found other delights, for just within the city he entered a piazza, just like a Roman piazza, although much smaller; and in the middle of the piazza there was a fountain, and standing in the fountain was the marble representation of a boy with a dolphin, and from the dolphin's mouth a stream of clear water issued.

'I do hope you like it,' a voice said from behind Carmody's left shoulder.

Carmody did not jump with alarm. He did not even whirl around. He had become accustomed to voices speaking from behind his back. Sometimes it seemed to him that a great many things in the galaxy liked to approach him that way.

'It's very nice,' Carmody said.

'I constructed it and put it there myself,' the voice said. 'It seemed to me that a fountain, despite the antiquity of the concept, is aesthetically functional. And this piazza, with its benches and shady chestnut trees, is copied from a Bolognese model. Again, I did not inhibit myself with the fear of being old-fashioned. The true artist, it seems to me, uses what he finds necessary, be it a thousand years old or one second new.'

'I applaud your sentiment,' Carmody said. 'Permit me to introduce myself. I am Thomas Carmody.' He turned, smiling, his hand outstretched. But there was no one behind his left shoulder, or behind his right shoulder, either. There was no one in the piazza, nobody at all in sight.

'Forgive me,' the voice said. 'I didn't mean to startle you. I thought you knew.'

'Knew what?' Carmody asked.

'Knew about me.'

'Well, I don't,' Carmody said. 'Who are you and where are you speaking from?'

'I am the voice of the city,' the voice said. 'Or to put it another way, I am the city itself, the veritable city, speaking to you.'

'Is that a fact?' Carmody said sardonically. 'Yes,' he answered himself, 'I suppose it is a fact. So all right, you're a city. Big deal!'

The fact was, Carmody was annoyed. He had encountered too many entities of great magnitude and miraculous power. He had been one-upped from one end of the galaxy to the other. Forces, creations and personifications had jumped out at him without cessation, causing him time and time again to lose his cool. Carmody was a reasonable man; he knew there was an interstellar pecking order, and that humans did not rate very high on it. But he was also a proud man. He believed that a man stood for something, if only for himself. A man couldn't very well go around all the time saying 'Oh!' and 'Ah!' and 'Bless my soul!' to the various inhuman entities that surrounded him; he couldn't do that and keep any self-respect. Carmody cared more than a little for his self-respect. It was, at this point, one of the few things he still possessed.

Therefore, Carmody turned away from the fountain and strolled across the piazza like a man who conversed with cities every day of his life, and who was slightly bored with the whole thing. He walked down various streets and up certain avenues. He glanced into store windows and noted the size of houses. He paused in front of statuary, but only briefly.

'Well?' the city said after a while.

'Well what?' Carmody answered instantly.

'What do you think of me?'

'You're OK,' Carmody said.

'Only OK?'

'Look,' Carmody said, 'a city is a city. When you've seen one, you've pretty much seen them all.'

'That's untrue!' the city said, with some show of pique. 'I am distinctly different from other cities. I am unique.'

'Are you indeed?' Carmody said scornfully. 'To me you look like a conglomeration of badly assembled parts. You've got an Italian piazza, a couple Greek-type statues, a row of Tudor houses, an old-style New York tenement, a California hot-dog stand shaped like a tugboat, and God knows what else. What's so unique about that?'

'The combination of those forms into a meaningful entity is unique,' the city said. 'I present variety within a framework of inner consistency. These older forms are not anachronisms, you understand; they are representative styles of living and as such are appropriate in a well-wrought machine for living.'

'That's *your* opinion,' Carmody said. 'Do you have a name, by the way?'

'Of course,' the city said. 'My name is Bellwether. I am an incorporated township in the State of New Jersey. Would you care to have some coffee and perhaps a sandwich or some fresh fruit?'

'The coffee sounds good,' Carmody said. He allowed the voice of Bellwether to guide him around the corner to an open-air café. The café was called 'O You Kid' and was a replica of a Gay Nineties saloon, right down to the Tiffany lamps and the cut-glass chandelier and the player piano. Like everything else that Carmody had seen in the city, it was spotlessly clean, but without people.

'Nice atmosphere, don't you think?' Bellwether asked.

'Campy,' Carmody pronounced. 'OK if you like that sort of thing.' A foaming mug of cappuccino was lowered to his table on a stainless-steel tray. 'But at least the service is good,' Carmody added. He sipped the coffee.

'Good?' Bellwether asked.

'Yes, very good.'

'I rather pride myself on my coffee,' Bellwether said quietly. 'And on my cooking. Wouldn't you like a little something? An omelette, perhaps, or a soufflé?'

'Nothing,' Carmody said firmly. He leaned back in his chair and said, 'So you're a model city, huh?'

'Yes, that is what I have the honour to be,' Bellwether said. 'I am the most recent of all model cities and, I believe, the most satisfactory. I was conceived by a joint study group from Yale and the University of Chicago, who were working on a Rockefeller fellowship. Most of my practical details were devised by MIT, although some special sections of me came from Princeton and from the RAND Corporation. My actual construction was a General Electric project, and the money was procured by grants from the Ford Foundation, as well as several other institutions I am not at liberty to mention.'

'Interesting sort of history,' Carmody said, with unbearable nonchalance. 'That's a Gothic cathedral across the street, isn't it?'

'Yes, completely Gothic,' said Bellwether. 'Also, interdenominational and open to all faiths, with a designed seating capacity for three hundred people.'

'That doesn't seem like much for a building that size.'

'It's not, of course. But my idea was to combine awesomeness with cosiness. Many people liked it.'

'Where are the people, by the way?' Carmody asked. 'I haven't seen any.'

'They have left,' Bellwether said mournfully. 'They have all departed.'

'Why?' Carmody asked.

Bellwether was silent for a while, then said, 'There was a breakdown in city-community relations. A misunderstanding, really; or perhaps I should say, an unfortunate series of misunderstandings. I suspect that rabble-rousers played a part in the exodus.'

'But what *happened*, precisely?'

'I don't know,' Bellwether said. 'I really don't know. One day they simply all left. Just like that! But I'm sure they'll be back.'

'I wonder,' Carmody said.

'I am convinced of it,' Bellwether said. 'But for the nonce, why don't you stay here, Mr Carmody?'

'Me? I really don't think –'

'You appear to be travel-weary,' Bellwether said. 'I'm sure the rest would do you good.'

'I have been on the move a lot recently,' Carmody admitted.

'Who knows, you might find that you liked it here,' Bellwether said. 'And in any event, you would have the unique experience of having the most modern, up-to-date city in the world at your service.'

'That does sound interesting,' Carmody said. 'I'll have to think about it.'

He was intrigued by the city of Bellwether. But he was also apprehensive. He wished he knew exactly what had happened to the city's occupants.

Chapter 23

At Bellwether's insistence, Carmody went to sleep that night in the sumptuous bridal suite of the King George V Hotel. He awoke in the morning refreshed and grateful. He had been in great need of a cessation of consciousness.

Bellwether served him breakfast on the terrace and played a brisk Haydn quartet while Carmody ate. The air was delicious; if Bellwether hadn't told him, Carmody would never have guessed it was filtered. The temperature and humidity were also exquisitely satisfactory. In front of the terrace was a splendid view of Bellwether's western quarter – a pleasing jumble of Chinese pagodas, Venetian footbridges, Japanese canals, a green hill, a Corinthian temple, a parking lot, a Norman tower, and much else besides.

'You have a splendid view,' he told the city.

'I'm so glad you appreciate it,' Bellwether replied.

'Style was a problem that was argued from various positions from the day of my inception. One group held for consistency: a harmonious group of shapes blending into a harmonious whole. But that had been tried before. Quite a few model cities are like that. They are uniformly dull, artificial entities created by one man or one committee, unlike real cities.'

'You're sort of artificial yourself, aren't you?' Carmody asked.

'Of course! But I do not pretend to be anything else. I am not a fake "city of the future" or a mock-Florentine bastard. I am a conglomerate entity. I am supposed to be interesting and stimulating, as well as being functional and practical.'

'Bellwether, to me you look OK,' Carmody said. 'Do all model cities talk like you?'

'No,' Bellwether said. 'Most cities up to now, model or otherwise, have never said a word. But their occupants didn't like it. They didn't like a city that did things without saying a word. The city seemed too huge, too masterful, too soulless. That is why I was created with an artificial consciousness.'

'I see,' Carmody said.

'I wonder if you do. The artificial consciousness personalizes me, which is very important in an age of depersonalization. It enables me to be truly responsive. It permits me to be creative in my reactions to the demands of my occupants. We can reason with each other, my occupants and I. By carrying on an incessant and meaningful dialogue, we can help each other in the creation of a truly viable urban environment. We can modify each other without any significant loss of individuality.'

'It sounds fine,' Carmody said. 'Except, of course, that you don't have anyone here to carry on a dialogue with.'

'That is the only flaw in the scheme,' Bellwether admitted. 'But for the present, I have you.'

'Yes, you have me,' Carmody said, and wondered why the words rang unpleasantly on his ear.

'And, naturally, you have me,' Bellwether said. 'It's a reciprocal relationship, which is the only kind worth having. But now, my dear Carmody, suppose I show you around myself. Then we can get you settled in and regularized.'

'And what?'

'I didn't mean it the way it sounded,' Bellwether said. 'It simply is an unfortunate scientific expression. But you understand, I'm sure, that; a reciprocal relationship necessitates obligations on the part of both involved parties. It couldn't very well be otherwise, could it?'

'Not unless it was a *laissez-faire* relationship,'

'We're trying to get away from all that,' Bellwether said. '*Laissez-faire* becomes a doctrine of the emotions, you know, and leads nonstop to anomie. If you will just come this way . . .'

Carmody went where he was told and beheld the excellencies of Bellwether. He toured the power plant, the water-filtration system, the industrial park, and the light-industries section. He saw the children's park and the Odd Fellows Hall. He walked through a museum and an art gallery, a concert hall and a theatre, and a bowling alley, a billiards parlour, a Go-Kart track, and a movie theatre. He became tired and footsore and wanted to stop. But Bellwether insisted upon showing itself off and Carmody had to look at the five-storey American Express building, the Portuguese synagogue, the statue of Buckminster Fuller, the Greyhound Bus Station, and several other attractions.

At last it was over. Carmody concluded that the wonders of the model city were no better and no worse than the wonders of the galaxy. Beauty was really in the eye of the beholder, except for a small part that was in his feet.

'A little lunch now?' Bellwether asked.

'Fine,' Carmody said.

He was guided to the fashionable Rochambeau Café, where he began with *potage aux petits pois* and ended with petits fours.

'What about a nice Gruyère to finish it off?' Bellwether asked.

'No, thanks,' Carmody said. 'I'm full. I'm too full, as a matter of fact.'

'But cheese isn't filling. A nice Camembert?'

'I couldn't possibly.'

'Perhaps a few assorted fruits. *Very* refreshing to the palate.'

'It's not my palate that needs refreshing,' Carmody said.

'At least an apple, a pear, and a couple of grapes?'

'Thanks, no.'

'A couple of cherries?'

'No, no, no!'

'A meal isn't complete without a little fruit,' Bellwether said.

'My meal is,' Carmody said.

'There are important vitamins which only fresh fruit can give you.'

'I'll just have to struggle along without them.'

'Perhaps half an orange, which I will peel for you? Citrus fruits have no bulk at all.'

'I couldn't possibly.'

'Not even one quarter of an orange? If I take out all the pits?'

'Most decidedly not.'

'It would make me feel better,' Bellwether said. 'I have a completion compulsion, you know, and no meal is complete without a piece of fruit.'

'No! No! No!'

'All right, don't get so excited,' Bellwether said. 'If you don't like the sort of food I serve, that's up to you.'

'But I do like it!'

'Then if you like it so much, why won't you eat some fruit?'

'Enough,' Carmody said. 'Give me a couple grapes.'

'I wouldn't want to force anything on you.'

'You're not forcing. Give me, please.'

'You're quite sure?'

'Gimme!' Carmody shouted.

'So take,' Bellwether said, and produced a magnificent bunch of muscatel grapes. Carmody ate them all. They were very good.

'Excuse me,' Bellwether said. 'What are you doing?'

Carmody sat upright and opened his eyes. 'I was taking a little nap,' he said. 'Is there anything wrong with that?'

'What should be wrong with a perfectly natural thing like that?' Bellwether said.

'Thank you,' Carmody said, and closed his eyes again.

'But why nap in a chair?' Bellwether asked.

'Because I'm *in* a chair, and I'm already half asleep.'

'You'll get a crick in your back,' Bellwether warned him.

'Don't care,' Carmody mumbled, his eyes still closed.

'Why not take a proper nap? Over here, on the couch?'

'I'm already napping comfortably where I am.'

'You're not really comfortable,' Bellwether pointed out. 'The human anatomy is not constructed for sleeping sitting up.'

'At the moment, mine is,' Carmody said.

'It's not. Why not try the couch?'

'The chair is fine.'

'But the couch is finer. Just try it, please, Carmody. Carmody?'

'Eh? What's that?' Carmody said, waking up.

'The couch. I really think you should rest on the couch.'

'All right!' Carmody said, struggling to his feet. 'Where is this couch?'

He was guided out of the restaurant, down the street, around the corner, and into a building marked 'The Snoozerie.' There were a dozen couches. Carmody went to the nearest.

'Not that one,' Bellwether said. 'It's got a bad spring.'

'It doesn't matter,' Carmody said. 'I'll sleep around it.'

'That will result in a cramped posture.'

'Christ!' Carmody said, getting to his feet. 'Which would you recommend?'

'This one back here,' Bellwether said. 'It's king-size, the best in the place. The yield-point of the mattress has been scientifically determined. The pillows –'

'Right, fine, good,' Carmody said, lying down on the indicated couch.

'Shall I play you some soothing music?'

'Don't bother.'

'Just as you wish. I'll put out the lights, then.'

'Fine.'

'Would you like a blanket? I control the temperature here, of course, but sleepers often get a subjective impression of chilliness.'

'It doesn't matter! Leave me alone!'

'All right!' Bellwether said. 'I'm not doing this for myself, you know. Personally, I never sleep.'

'OK, sorry,' Carmody said.

'That's perfectly all right,' Bellwether said.

There was a long silence. Then Carmody sat up.

'What's the matter?' Bellwether asked.

'Now I can't sleep,' Carmody said.

'Try closing your eyes and consciously relaxing every muscle in your body, starting with the big toe and working upward to –'

'I can't sleep!' Carmody shouted.

'Maybe you weren't very sleepy to begin with,' Bellwether suggested. 'But at least you could close your eyes and try to get a little rest. Won't you do that for me?'

'No!' Carmody said. 'I'm not sleepy and I don't need a rest.'

'Stubborn!' Bellwether said. 'Do what you like. I've tried my best.'

'Yeah,' Carmody said, getting to his feet and walking out of The Snoozerie.

Carmody stood on a little curved bridge and looked over a blue lagoon.

'This is a copy of the Rialto bridge in Venice,' Bellwether said. 'Scaled down, of course.'

'I know,' Carmody said. 'I read the sign.'

'It's rather enchanting, isn't it?'

'Sure, it's fine,' Carmody said, lighting a cigarette.

'You're doing a lot of smoking,' Bellwether pointed out.

'I know. I feel like smoking.'

'As your medical adviser, I must point out that the link between smoking and lung cancer is conclusive.'

'I know.'

'If you switched to a pipe, your chances would be improved,'

'I don't like pipes.'

'What about a cigar, then?'

'I don't like cigars.' He lit another cigarette.

'That's your third cigarette in five minutes,' Bellwether said.

'Goddamn it, I'll smoke as much and as often as I please!' Carmody shouted.

'Well, of course you will!' Bellwether said. 'I was merely trying to advise you for your own good. Would you want me to simply stand by and not say a word while you destroyed yourself?'

'Yes,' Carmody said.

'I can't believe you mean that. There is an ethical imperative involved here. Man can act against his best interests, but a machine is not allowed that degree of perversity.'

'Get off my back,' Carmody said sullenly. 'Quit pushing me around.'

'Pushing you around? My dear Carmody, have I coerced you in any way? Have I done any more than advise you?'

'Maybe not. But you talk too much.'

'Perhaps I don't talk enough,' Bellwether said. 'To judge from the response I get.'

'You talk too much,' Carmody repeated, and lit a cigarette.

'That is your fourth cigarette in five minutes.'

Carmody opened his mouth to bellow an insult. Then he changed his mind and walked away.

★

'What's this?' Carmody asked.

'It's a candy machine,' Bellwether told him.

'It doesn't look like one.'

'Still, it is one. This design is a modification of a design by Saarinomen for a silo. I have miniaturized it, of course, and –'

'It still doesn't look like a candy machine. How do you work it?'

'It's very simple. Push the red button. Now wait. Press down one of those levers on Row A; now press the green button. There!'

A Babe Ruth bar slid into Carmody's hand.

'Huh,' Carmody said. He stripped off the paper and bit into the bar. 'Is this a real Babe Ruth bar or a copy of one?' he asked.

'It's a real one. I had to subcontract the candy concession because of the pressure of work.'

'Huh,' Carmody said, letting the candy wrapper slip out of his fingers.

'That,' Bellwether said, 'is an example of the kind of thoughtlessness I always encounter.'

'It's just a piece of paper,' Carmody said, turning and looking at the candy wrapper lying on the spotless street.

'Of course it's just a piece of paper,' Bellwether said. 'But multiply it by a hundred thousand inhabitants and what do you have?'

'A hundred thousand pieces of paper,' Carmody answered at once.

'I don't consider that funny,' Bellwether said. 'You wouldn't want to live in the midst of all that paper, I can assure you. You'd be the first to complain if this street were strewn with rubbish. But do you do your share? Do you even clean up after yourself? Of course not! You leave it to me, even though I have to run all the other functions of the city, night and day, without even Sundays off.'

'Must you go on so?' Carmody asked. 'I'll pick it up.'

He bent down to pick up the candy wrapper. But just before his fingers could close on it, a pincer arm shot out of the nearest sewer, snatched the paper away and vanished from sight.

'It's all right,' Bellwether said. 'I'm used to cleaning up after people. I do it all the time.'

'Yuh,' said Carmody.

'Nor do I expect any gratitude.'

'I'm grateful, I'm grateful!' Carmody said.

'No, you're not,' Bellwether said.

'So OK, maybe I'm not. What do you want me to say?'

'I don't want you to say anything,' Bellwether said.

'Let us consider the incident closed.'

'Had enough?' Bellwether said, after dinner.

'Plenty,' Carmody said.

'You didn't eat much.'

'I ate all I wanted. It was very good.'

'If it was so good, why didn't you eat more?'

'Because I couldn't hold any more.'

'If you hadn't spoiled your appetite with that candy bar . . .'

'Goddamn it, the candy bar didn't spoil my appetite! I just –'

'You're lighting a cigarette,' Bellwether said.

'Yeah,' Carmody said.

'Couldn't you wait a little longer?'

'Now look,' Carmody said. 'Just what in hell do you –'

'But we have something more important to talk about,' Bellwether said quickly. 'Have you thought about what you're going to do for a living?'

'I haven't really had much time to think about it.'

'Well, I *have* been thinking about it. It would be nice if you became a doctor.'

'Me? I'd have to take special college courses, then get into medical school, and so forth.'

'I can arrange all that,' Bellwether said.

'Not interested.'

'Well . . . what about law?'

'Never.'

'Engineering is an excellent line.'

'Not for me.'

'What about accounting?'

'Not on your life.'

'What do you want to be, then?'

'A jet pilot,' Carmody said impulsively.

'Oh, come now!'

'I'm quite serious.'

'I don't even have an airfield here.'

'Then I'll pilot somewhere else.'

'You're only saying that to spite me!'

'Not at all,' Carmody said. 'I want to be a pilot, I really do. I've *always* wanted to be a pilot! Honest I have!'

There was a long silence. Then Bellwether said, 'The choice is entirely up to you.' This was said in a voice like death.

*

'Where are you going?'

'Out for a walk,' Carmody said.

'At 9:30 in the evening?'

'Sure. Why not?'

'I thought you were tired.'

'That was quite some time ago.'

'I see. And I also thought that perhaps you could sit here and we could maybe have a nice chat.'

'How about if we talk when I get back?' Carmody asked.

'No, it doesn't matter,' Bellwether said.

'The walk doesn't matter,' Carmody said, sitting down. 'Come on, we'll talk.'

'I no longer care to talk,' Bellwether said. 'Please go for your walk.'

'Well, good night,' Carmody said.

'I beg your pardon?'

'I said, "good night."'

'You're going to sleep?'

'Sure. It's late, I'm tired.'

'You're going to sleep now, just like that?'

'Well, why not?'

'No reason at all,' Bellwether said, 'except that you have forgotten to wash.'

'Oh . . . I guess I did forget. I'll wash in the morning.'

'How long is it since you've had a bath?'

'Too long. I'll take one in the morning.'

'Wouldn't you feel better if you took one right now?'

'No.'

'Even if I drew the bath for you?'

'No! Goddamn it, no! I'm going to sleep!'

'Do exactly as you please,' Bellwether said. 'Don't wash, don't study, don't eat a balanced diet. But also, don't blame me.'

'Blame you? For what?'

'For anything,' Bellwether said.

'Yes. But what did you have in mind, specifically?'

'It isn't important.'

'Then why did you bring it up in the first place?'

'I was only thinking of you,' Bellwether said.

'I realize that.'

'You must know that it can't benefit *me* if you wash or not.'

'I'm aware of that.'

'When one cares,' Bellwether went on, 'when one feels one's responsibilities, it is not nice to hear oneself sworn at.'

'I didn't swear at you.'

'Not this time. But earlier today you did.'

'Well . . . I was nervous.'

'That's because of the smoking.'

'Don't start that again!'

'I won't,' Bellwether said. 'Smoke like a furnace. What does it matter to me? They're your lungs, aren't they?'

'Damned right,' Carmody said, lighting a cigarette.

'But my failure,' Bellwether said.

'No, no,' Carmody said. 'Don't say it, please don't!'

'Forget I said it,' Bellwether said.

'All right.'

'Sometimes I get overzealous.'

'Sure.'

'And it's especially difficult because I'm right. I *am* right, you know.'

'I know,' Carmody said. 'You're right, you're right, you're always right. Right right right right right –'

'Don't overexcite yourself before bedtime,' Bellwether said. 'Would you care for a glass of milk?'

'No.'

'You're sure?'

Carmody put his hands over his eyes. He felt very strange. He also felt extremely guilty, fragile, dirty, unhealthy, and sloppy. He felt generally and irrevocably bad, and he knew that it would always be this way.

From somewhere within him he found strength. He shouted, 'Seethwright!'

'Who are you shouting to?' Bellwether asked.

'Seethwright! Where are you?'

'How have I failed you?' Bellwether asked. 'Just tell me how!'

'Seethwright!' Carmody wailed. 'Come and get me! This is the wrong Earth!'

There was a snap, crackle and pop, and Carmody was somewhere else.

Chapter 24

Whoosh! Krrrunch! Kerpow! Here we are somewhere, but who knows where and when and which? Surely not Carmody, who found himself in a persuasive city much like New York. *Much* like; but was it?

'*Is* this New York?' Carmody asked himself.

'How the hell should I know?' a voice answered promptly.

'It was a rhetorical question,' Carmody said.

'I am quite aware of that; but, since I have my rhetorician's papers, I answered it.'

Carmody looked around and saw that the voice had come from a large black umbrella in his left hand. He asked, 'Are you my Prize?'

'Well, of course I am,' the Prize said. 'I don't suppose I look like a Shetland pony, do I?'

'Where were you earlier, when I was in that model city?'

'I was taking a short, well-earned vacation,' the Prize said. 'And there's no use your complaining about it. Vacation time is stipulated in the contract between the Amalgamated Prizes of the Galaxy and the Recipient's League.'

'I wasn't complaining,' Carmody said. 'I just. . . Forget it. This place certainly looks like my Earth. It looks like New York, in fact.'

He was in a city. There was heavy traffic, both human and vehicular. There were many theatres, many frankfurter stands, many people. There were many stores which proclaimed that they were going out of business and selling their entire stock regardless of cost. Neon signs flashed everywhere. There were many restaurants, most prominent of which were The Westerner, The Southerner, The Easterner, and The Northerner; all of these had specials on steak and shoe-string potatoes. But there was also The Nor'easterner, The Sou'wester, The East-by-Northeast, and the West-by-Northwest. A movie theatre across the street was featuring *The Apocrypha* (Bigger and Stranger than The Bible), with a cast of thousands. Near it was the Omphalos Discothèque wherein a folk-rock group calling itself The Shits played raucous music, which was danced to by immature virgins in middleless dresses.

'Lots of action,' Carmody said, wetting his lips.

'I hear only the jangle of cash registers,' the Prize said, in a heavily moralistic voice.

'Don't be stuffy,' Carmody said. 'I think I'm home.'

'I hope not,' the Prize said. 'This place gets on my nerves. Please look around you and make sure. Remember, similitude need not imply exactitude.'

There was an IRT subway entrance in front of him. He saw that he was at Fiftieth Street and Broadway. Yes, he was home. He walked briskly to the subway and went down the stairs. It was familiar, exciting and saddening all at the same time. The marble walls were damp with ichor, and the gleaming monorail came out of one tunnel and disappeared into another . . .

'Oh,' Carmody muttered.

'How's that?' the Prize asked.

'Never mind,' Carmody said. 'On second thoughts, I think I'll take a little stroll in the streets.' He began to retrace his footsteps, moving quietly towards the rectangle of sky framed in the entrance. A crowd had formed, blocking his way. Carmody pushed through them, and the crowd pushed him back. The wet walls of the subway began to tremble, then to convulse rhythmically. The gleaming monorail pulled free of its stanchions, curled back on itself like a brazen tongue, and flicked out towards him. Carmody ran, bowling over the people who stood in his way. He was dimly aware that they rolled immediately to their feet, as though they had weighted bases. The marble pavement beneath him grew soft, syrupy. His feet were sticking, the figures were close around him, and the monorail was poised over his head.

Carmody shouted, 'Seethwright! Get me out of this!'

'Me, too!' the Prize shouted.

'Me, too!' screamed the cunning predator; for it was he and none other, cleverly disguised as a subway, into whose mouth Carmody had strayed.

Nothing happened. Carmody had the terrible feeling that Seethwright was perhaps out to lunch, or on the toilet, or answering a telephone. The blue rectangle of sky became smaller as the exit sealed itself. The figures around him lost their resemblance to humans. The walls turned a purplish-red, began to heave and tremble, then to contract. The slender monorail curled hungrily around Carmody's feet. Within the predator's body, vast ululations were followed by protracted slaverings. (Carmody-eaters are notoriously piggish and lacking in any table manners.)

'Help!' Carmody screamed, as digestive juices ate away the soles of his shoes. 'Seethwright, help me!'

'Help him, help him!' the Prize sobbed. 'Or, if that seems too difficult, help me! Get me out of here and I will take advertisements in the leading newspapers, convene, committees, form action groups, carry posters on the streets, all to the purpose of insuring that Carmody does not go unavenged. And I further pledge myself to –'

'Stop babbling,' a voice said, which Carmody recognized as belonging to Seethwright. 'It's disgraceful. As for you, Mr Carmody, you must, in future, make up your mind *before* stepping into the mouth of your predator. My office is not set up for hair's-breadth rescues.'

'But you will save me this time, won't you?' Carmody begged. 'Won't you? Won't you?'

'It is already done,' Seethwright said. And when Carmody looked around, he saw that it was indeed already done.

Chapter 25

Seethwright must have mishandled the transition, for, after a brief blank spell, Carmody found himself in the back seat of a taxi. He was in a city very much like New York, and he seemed to be in the middle of a conversation.

'What didja say?' the driver asked.

'I didn't say anything,' Carmody replied.

'Oh. I thought you were saying something. Well, what *I* was saying is, I was saying that's the new Flammarion building over there.'

'I know,' Carmody heard himself say. 'I helped build it.'

'Is that a fact? Some job! But now you're finished, huh?'

'Yes,' Carmody said. He took the cigarette out of his mouth and frowned at it. 'I'm finished with these cigarettes, too.' He shook his head and threw the cigarette out of the window. These words and actions seemed perfectly natural to one part of him (the active consciousness). But another part of him (the reflective consciousness) was watching with considerable amusement.

'Well, why didn't you say so?' the cabby said. 'Here, try one of mine.'

Carmody looked at the open pack in the driver's hand. 'You smoke Kools, eh?'

'It's my regular smoke,' the cabby said. 'Kools have that light touch of menthol and the taste that's right!'

Carmody raised both eyebrows to show disbelief. Nevertheless, he accepted the pack, extracted a coffin nail and lit up. The smiling cabby was watching him in the rearview mirror. Carmody inhaled, looked surprised and pleased, exhaled slowly and luxuriously.

'Hey!' Carmody said. 'You got something there!'

The driver nodded sagely. 'A lot of us Kool smokers think so . . . Here we are, sir. The Waldorf-Astoria.'

Carmody paid and began to step out. The cabby leaned back, still smiling. 'Hey, mister,' he said. 'How about my Kools?'

'Oh!' Carmody said. He gave back the pack. He and the cabby smiled at each other. Then the cabby drove off and Carmody stood in front of the Waldorf-Astoria.

He was wearing a sturdy Burberry topcoat. He could tell this by reading the label, which, instead of being inside the collar, was sewn securely to the outside of his right sleeve. Now that he looked, he saw that all his labels were outside: anyone could tell that he had on a Van Heusen shirt, a Countess Mara necktie, a Hart, Schaffner & Marx suit, Van Camp socks, and Lloyd & Haig cordovans. Upon his head was a Borsolino made by Raimu of Milan. His hands were encased in deerskin gloves from L.L. Bean. His wrist was covered by a self-winding chronometer (Audemars Piccard) which had a slide rule, a timer, an elapsed-time indicator, a calendar, and an alarm; all this in addition to keeping time within a guaranteed accuracy of plus or minus six seconds a year.

Finally, he smelled faintly of Oak Moss men's cologne from Abercrombie & Fitch.

He considered it a *fairly good* outfit, though by no means first-rate. It would pass muster, but he expected more of himself. He was ambitious, he planned to move up, he expected to become the sort of man who serves Chivas Regal on days other than Christmas, wears Brooks Brothers shirts, blazers from F. R. Tripler, uses Onyx after-shave lotion by Lentheric, slips into Country Warmer jackets by Paul Stuart . . .

But he would need a class A-AA-AAA Consumer Rating for goods like those, instead of his commonplace B-BB-AAAA which a mishap of birth had stuck him with. He *needed* that rating! Wasn't he good enough? Why, damn it, at Stanford he'd been first in his class in Consumer Techniques! His Use-Index for three years now had been in the ninetieth percentile! His car, a Dodge Ferret, was immaculate! He could cite other examples.

Why hadn't they moved him up?

Was it possible that they did not have their eye on him?

Carmody quickly put such heretical thoughts out of his mind. He had more immediate concerns. Today he had a thankless task before him. What he had to do in the next hour might well cost him his job, in which case he would be relegated to the empty-faced ranks of the proletarian users of Irregular Oriental Merchandise Seconds (IOMS).

It was still early, but he needed fortification for the

ordeal ahead. He walked into the Men's Bar of the Waldorf.

He caught the bartender's eye. Quickly, before the man could speak, Carmody said, 'Hey, friend, do it again.' The fact that the man had not done it for him previously, and therefore, technically, could not do it again, was of no significance.

'Here you go, Mac,' the bartender said, smiling. 'Ballantine's got the deep-brewed flavour and the taste that's right.'

Carmody knew that he should have said that himself. He had been caught napping. He sipped his beer thoughtfully.

'Hey, Tom?'

Carmody turned around. There was Nate Steen from Leonia, New Jersey, an old friend and neighbour, drinking a Coke. 'It's funny,' Steen said, 'but did you ever notice? Things go better with Coke.'

Carmody was caught without a line. He drained off his beer at a gulp and called to the bartender, 'Hey, friend, do it again!' It was a poor expedient, but better than nothing at all. 'What's new?' he asked Steen.

'Wife's gone on vacation. She decided to come on down to Miami and sneak a week via American Airways, number one to the sun.'

'That's great,' Carmody said. 'I just sent Helen to Nassau; and if you think the Bahamas are lovely from the air, wait until you land. And do you know, I was asking her just the other night why, in this fast-moving world of ours, would anyone want to take the time for an ocean voyage to Europe? And she said –'

'Nice idea,' Steen interrupted. He had a perfect right, of course; the Holland-American bit was entirely too long for verisimilitude. 'Now me, I thought I'd pack us all off to Marlboro Country.'

'Fine thought,' Carmody said, 'after all –'

' – you really *do* get a lot to like in a Marlboro,' Steen finished (his privilege: he had begun the plug).

'Sure,' Carmody said. Hastily he slopped down his beer and called out, 'Hey, friend, do it again! Ballantine beer!' But he knew that he wasn't holding up his end. What on earth was wrong with him? For this very moment, this particular situation, there was an obligatory dialogue. But he couldn't remember, he couldn't seem to find it . . .

Steen, calm and collected with new improved ice-blue Secret clinging to his hairy armpits, came to it first. 'With our wives away,' he chuckled, 'we get to do the wash.'

Beaten to the punch! Carmody could do no more than to string along. 'Yeh,' he said. He gave a hollow laugh. 'Remember that stuff about "my wash is whiter than yours"?'

Both men indulged in, scornful laughter. Then Steen looked at his shirt, looked at Carmody's shirt, frowned, raised his eyebrows, opened his mouth, portrayed disbelief, incredulity, amazement.

'Hey!' Steen said. 'My shirt is whiter than yours!'

'Gee, so it is!' Carmody said, not bothering to look. 'That's funny. We used the same model of washing machine set for the same cycle. And we also used the same bleach . . . Didn't we?'

'I used that Clorox stuff,' Steen said carelessly.

'Clorox,' Carmody said thoughtfully. 'Yeah, that's gotta be it! *My bleach was too weak!*'

He portrayed mock exasperation while Steen feigned triumph. Carmody thought of ordering another beer, but he hadn't enjoyed the last two. He decided that Steen was too quick for him.

Carmody paid for the beers with his American Express credit card and then continued to his office, which was on the fifty-first floor of 666 Fifth Avenue. He greeted his fellow workers with democratic camaraderie. Several people tried to involve him in their gambits, but he ignored them. Carmody knew that his situation, life-positionwise, was desperate. He had thought about his alternatives all last night. Worry had brought on an acute migraine and an upset stomach, and he had almost missed the Charleston contest. But his wife, Helen (who hadn't really gone on vacation), had given him an Alka-Seltzer, which had fixed him up in a jiffy, and they had gone as planned and had taken first prize thanks to Alka-Seltzer. But the problem had remained. And when Helen told him, at three in the morning, that Tommy and little Tinker had had 32 per cent fewer cavities this year over last, he had replied, 'Do you know . . . I'll bet it's the Crest!' But his heart hadn't been in it, although it bad been sweet of Helen to feed him the line.

He knew that no wife could feed her husband enough lines to make any real difference. If you wanted to advance in the Consumer Ratings, if you wanted to show yourself worthy of the things that counted in life – a Tech-built Swiss-type chalet deep in the Untrammelled

Wilderness of Maine, for example, and a Porsche 911S, which people who considered themselves a breed apart purchased, and an Ampex for people who couldn't be bothered with anything less than the best ... well, if you wanted that sort of thing, you had to deserve it. Money wasn't enough, social position wasn't enough, simpleminded perseverance wasn't enough. You had to prove that you really *were* of that Breed Apart for whom those goods were intended. You had to risk everything in order to gain everything.

'By jingo!' Carmody said to himself, striking his right fist into the palm of his left hand, 'I said I'd do it and I will do it!' And he boldly advanced to the door of Mr Übermann, his boss, and boldy threw open the door.

The room was empty. Mr Übermann had not arrived yet.

Carmody entered the office. He would wait. His jaw was tight, his lips were compressed, and three vertical lines had appeared between his eyes. He fought to keep himself under control. Übermann would be here any moment. And when he came, Tom Carmody would say to him, 'Mr Übermann, you could have me fired for this but you've got bad breath.' He would pause, '*Bad breath.*'

How simple it seemed in contemplation, how difficult in execution! Yet still, a man must stand up, must fight for cleanliness and its extensions, must scramble for advancement. At this very moment, Carmody knew, the eyes of those half-legendary figures, the Manufacturers, were on him. If he were found worthy ...

'Morning, Carmody!' said Übermann, striding long-legged into the room. He was hawk-faced and handsome;

his temples were streaked with grey, a mark of privilege. His horn-rimmed glasses were a full three centimetres wider than Carmody's.

'Mr Übermann,' Carmody began in a quavering voice, 'you could have me fired for this –'

'Carmody,' the boss said, his diaphragmatic voice cutting through Carmody's weak chest tones as a Personna surgical-steel blade cuts through flab, 'today I have discovered the most amazing mouthwash. Scope, it is called. I believe my breath will be sweet for hours and hours.'

Carmody gave an ironic smile. What a fantastic coincidence! The boss had lucked into *the very mouthwash* that Carmody had been about to recommend. And it had worked! No longer did Mr Übermann's breath smell like a rubbish pit after a heavy rain. Now it was kissing-sweet (for girls, of course; Carmody himself was not interested in that sort of thing).

'Ever hear of it?' Übermann asked, and then left the office without waiting for an answer.

Carmody smiled even more ironically. He had failed again. And yet, he could feel an unmistakable sense of relief at the failure. Executive consumption was terribly trying, fantastically wearing. It was proper for a certain kind of man; but perhaps he was not that kind. Suppose he had made it? He could sense even now the regrets with which he would have given up his fifty-eighth-percentile consumption artifacts – his Raleigh coupons, his pigskin suede cap, his light-up Christmas tie, his Executive 'Quick-Trip' Business Case made of Skai, his KLH Model 24 stereo music system, and particularly his Lakeland top-of-the-line coat of imported, soft, supple New Zealand

Sueded shearling with the framed collar and lapels. And he would have had to dispose of all the rest of his dear, familiar objects as well.

'Sometimes things just work out right even when you think they're going wrong,' Carmody said to himself.

'They do? Just what in hell are you talking about?' Carmody replied to himself.

'Oh my God,' Carmody said to himself.

'Yeah,' Carmody's self answered Carmody. 'Acclimatized a little too quickly, didn't you?'

The two Carmodys looked at each other, compared notes and reached a conclusion. They coalesced.

'Seethwright!' Carmody shouted. 'Get me out of here!'

And Seethwright, that faithful man, did just that.

Chapter 26

With his usual punctuality, Seethwright sent him into another of Earth's probability-worlds. The transition was somewhat faster than instantaneous. It was so rapid, in fact, that time became ever so slightly retrograde, and Carmody had the eerie experience of giving a response before receiving the requisite stimulus. That was a contradiction, of course, a very small one, but still illegal. Seethwright took care of it by a standard obliteration procedure, and no one bothered to report it to the proper authorities. Its effect was nil except for the wear and tear on the space-time continuum, which Carmody didn't even notice.

Carmody found himself in a small town. Superficially, there was no problem of identification; this town was, or purported to be, Maplewood, New Jersey. Carmody had lived here between the ages of three and eighteen. This was his home, in so far as he had a home anywhere.

Or, more precisely, this was his home if it was what it seemed to be. But that remained to be proved.

He was standing on the corner of Durand Road and Maplewood Avenue, at the upper end of the town. Straight ahead was the shopping centre. Behind him were suburban streets rich in maple, oak, chestnut, elm, dogwood, and others. On his right was the Christian Science reading room. On his left was the railroad station.

'How now, voyager?' said a voice near his right thigh.

Carmody looked down and saw that he was carrying a fair-sized transistor radio. This, he knew at once, was the Prize.

'So you've come back,' Carmody said.

'Back? I never left.'

'I didn't see you in the last probability-world.'

'That's because you weren't looking very hard,' the Prize said. 'I was in your pocket in the form of a badly forged denarius.'

'How am I supposed to know that?' Carmody inquired.

'All you have to do is ask,' the Prize said. 'I am metamorphic by nature, and unpredictable even to myself. But you know that. Must I announce my presence each and every time we go somewhere?'

'It would help,' Carmody said.

'My pride would not allow such anxiety-ridden behaviour,' the Prize said firmly. 'I answer when called; when

175

not called, I do not assume that my presence is required. It was quite obvious that you didn't need me in the last probability-world. Therefore I took the opportunity to go to Sloklol's Restaurant for a decent feed, and then to the Haganicht Proparium to have my hide dry-cleaned, and then to Varinell's Solar Beacon Pub for a few drinks and a chat with a friend who happened to be in the neighbourhood, and then to –'

'How could you have done all that?' Carmody asked. 'I wasn't in that world for over half an hour.'

'I told you that our duration-flows are quite dissimilar,' the Prize said.

'Yes, so you did . . . But whereabouts are those places?'

'That would take quite a little while to explain,' the Prize said. 'As a matter of fact, it's easier to go there than to explain how to go there. Anyhow, they're the wrong kind of places for you.'

'Why?'

'Well . . . there are many reasons. But to cite only one, you would disapprove of the food eaten at the Solar Beacon Pub.'

'I've already seen you eat *orithi*,' Carmody reminded the Prize.

'Yes, of course. But *orithi* are an infrequent delicacy, morsels to be eaten once or twice in a lifetime. Whereas at the Solar Beacon Pub we Prizes and related species eat our staple subsistence diet.'

'And what is that?'

'You wouldn't want to know,' the Prize warned him.

'I do want to know.'

'I know that you *do* want to know; but after you hear, you will wish that you *didn't* know.'

'Out with it,' Carmody said. 'What is your staple diet?'

'All right, Mr Nosey,' the Prize said. 'But remember, you insisted upon knowing. My staple diet is myself.'

'Is what?'

'Myself. I said you wouldn't like it.'

'Your diet is yourself? You mean that you feast off your own body?'

'Precisely.'

'Damn it all,' Carmody said, 'aside from being repulsive, that's impossible. You can't live off yourself!'

'I can and I do,' the Prize said. 'And I'm quite proud of the fact. Morally, it is an outstanding example of personal freedom.'

'But it just isn't possible,' Carmody said. 'It violates the law of conservation of energy, or mass, or something like that. It sure as hell violates *some* natural law.'

'That's true, but only in a specialized sense,' the Prize said. 'When you come to examine the matter more closely, you can, I think, see that the impossibility is more apparent than real.'

'What in hell does *that* mean?'

'I don't know,' the Prize confessed. 'It's the answer in all our textbooks. Nobody ever questioned it before.'

'I want to get this straight,' Carmody said. 'Do you mean that you actually and literally *eat* portions of your own flesh?'

'Yes,' the Prize said. 'That's what I mean. Though you shouldn't confine it solely to my flesh. My liver is a tasty morsel, especially when chopped up with a hard-boiled egg and a little chicken fat. And my short ribs have served me well for a quick, casual sort of dinner; whereas my hams ought to be mild-cured for several weeks before –'

'Enough,' Carmody said.

'I'm sorry,' the Prize said.

'But just tell me this: how can your body provide enough food for your body (this sounds ridiculous) throughout a lifetime?'

'Well,' the Prize said thoughtfully, 'for one thing, I'm not a particularly heavy eater.'

'Perhaps I haven't made myself clear,' Carmody said. 'I mean, how can you provide bulk for your body if you are simultaneously *using* that bulk to feed your body with?'

'I'm afraid I don't quite understand that,' the Prize said.

'Let me try again. I mean this: if you consume your flesh –'

'And in fact I do,' the Prize put in.

'If you consume your flesh, and utilize the product of that consumption for the nutrition of that same flesh . . . Just a minute. If you weighed fifty pounds –'

'In point of fact, on my home planet I weigh precisely fifty pounds.'

'Excellent! Well, then. If you weigh fifty pounds, and, over the course of, let us say a year, consume forty pounds of yourself in order to support yourself, then what are you left with?'

'Ten pounds?' the Prize asked.

'Goddamn it, can't you see what I'm driving at? You

simply cannot nourish yourself *on* yourself for any length of time.'

'Why can't I?' the Prize asked.

'The Law of Diminishing Returns,' Carmody said, feeling lightheaded. 'Eventually there will be no more of you left for you to feed upon, and you will die.'

'I am quite aware of that,' the Prize said. 'But death is an inexorable fact, as true and unavoidable for the self-eaters as for the other-eaters. Everything and everybody dies, Carmody, no matter who or what it feeds upon.'

'You're putting me on!' Carmody howled. 'If you really did feed like that, you'd be dead in a week.'

'There are insects whose lifespan is but a single day,' the Prize said. 'Actually, we Prizes do rather well, longevity-wise. Remember, the more we consume, the less of us there is to be nourished, and the longer the remaining food lasts. And time is a great factor in autopredation. Most Prizes consume their future while in their infancy, thus leaving the actual corpus untouched until they have come into their maturity.'

'How do they consume their future?' Carmody asked.

'I can't explain how,' the Prize said. 'We simply do it, that's all. I, for example, gobbled up my substance for the ages eighty through ninety-two – senile years, by the way, which I wouldn't have enjoyed anyway. Now, by rationing my intake of myself, I think I can make it to my late seventies.'

'You're giving me a headache,' Carmody said. 'And you're also making me somewhat nauseous.'

'Indeed?' said the Prize indignantly. 'You've got a hell of a nerve to feel nauseous! You bloody butcher, how many animal sections have you consumed in your life-time? How many defenceless apples have you gobbled, how many heads of lettuce have you callously ripped from their beds? I have eaten an occasional *orithi*, to be sure; but at Judgement Day you will have to face the herds you have devoured. They will stand before you, Carmody, hundreds of brown-eyed cows, thousands of defenceless hens, endless rows of gentle little lambs; to say nothing of the forests of raped fruit trees and the acres of sav-aged gardens. I will pay for the *orithi* I have eaten; but how will you ever atone for the shrieking mounds of ani-mal and vegetable life that you have feasted upon? How, Carmody, how?'

'Shut up,' Carmody said.

'Oh, very well,' the Prize said sulkily.

'I eat because I must. It's part of my nature. That's all there is to it.'

'If you say so.'

'I damned well do say so! Now will you shut up and let me concentrate?'

'I won't say another word,' the Prize said, 'except to ask you what you are trying to concentrate on.'

'This place looks like my home town,' Carmody ex-plained. 'I'm trying to decide if it really is or not.'

'Surely that can't be so difficult,' the Prize said. 'I mean to say, one knows one's own home town, doesn't one?'

'No. I never looked at it closely while I lived here, and I didn't think about it much after I left.'

'If you can't figure out what is your home and what is not,' the Prize said, 'then no one can. I hope you real-ize that.'

'I realize it,' Carmody said. He began to walk slowly down Maplewood Avenue. He had the sudden terrible feeling that any decision he made would be wrong.

Chapter 27

Carmody looked as he walked, and observed as he looked. It seemed like the place he thought it should seem like. The Maplewood Theatre was on his right; today's feature was *The Saga of Elephantine*, an Italian-French adventure film directed by Jacques Marat, the brilliant young director who had given the world the deeply moving *Song of My Wounds* and the swiftly paced comedy *Paris Times Fourteen*. On the stage, for a limited engagement only, was the new vocal group, Iakonnen and the Fungi.

'Sounds like a fun film,' Carmody remarked.

'Not my sort of thing,' the Prize said.

Carmody stopped at Marvin's Haberdashery and looked in the window. He saw loafers and saddle shoes, hound's-tooth check jackets, wide, boldly patterned neckties, white shirts with spread collars. Next to it, at the stationery store, he glanced at the current *Colliers*, leafed through *Liberty*, noticed *Munsey's*, *Black Cat*, and *The Spy*. The morning edition of *The Sun* had just come out.

'Well?' the Prize asked. 'Is this the place?'

'I'm still checking,' Carmody said. 'But it looks pretty favourable so far.'

He crossed the street and looked into Edgar's Lunch-eonette. It hadn't changed. There was a pretty girl sitting at the counter, sipping a soda. Carmody recognized her at once.

'Lana Turner! Hey, how are you, Lana?'

'I'm fine, Tom,' Lana said. 'Long time no see.'

'I used to date her in high school,' he explained to the Prize as they walked on. 'It's funny how it all comes back to you.'

'I suppose so,' the Prize said doubtfully.

At the next corner, the intersection of Maplewood Avenue and South Mountain Road, there was a police-man. He was directing traffic, but he took time to grin at Carmody.

'That's Burt Lancaster,' Carmody said. 'He was all-state fullback on the best team Columbia High School ever had. And look, over there! That man going into the hardware store, the one who waved at me! That's Clifton Webb, our high-school principal. And down the block, do you see that blonde woman? That's Jean Harlow. She used to be the waitress at the Maplewood Restaurant.' He lowered his voice. 'Everybody said she was *fast.*'

'You seem to know a lot of people,' the Prize said.

'Well, of course I do! I was raised here! Miss Harlow is going into Pierre's Beauty Parlour.'

'Do you know Pierre, also?'

'Sure. He's a hairdresser now, but during the war he was in the French Resistance. What was his name again? Jean-Pierre Aumont, that's it! He married one of our local girls, Carole Lombard.'

'Interesting,' the Prize said in a bored voice.

'Well, it's interesting for me. Here comes a man I know . . . Good day, Mr Mayor.'

'Good day, Tom,' the man said, and tipped his hat and walked on.

'That's Fredric March, our mayor,' Carmody said. 'He's a tremendous person! I can still remember the debate between him and our local radical, Paul Muni. Boy, you never heard anything like it!'

'Hmm,' said the Prize. 'There is something strange about all this, Carmody. Something uncanny, something not right. Don't you feel it?'

'No, I don't,' Carmody said. 'I'm telling you, I grew up with these people, I know them better than I know myself. Hey, there's Paulette Goddard over there. She's the assistant librarian. Hi, Paulette!'

'Hi, Tom,' the woman said.

'I don't like this,' the Prize said.

'I never knew her very well,' Carmody said. 'She used to go with a boy from Millburn named Humphrey Bogart. He always wore bow ties, can you imagine that? He had a fight once with Lon Chaney, the school janitor. Licked him, too. I remember that because I was dating June Havoc at the time, and her best friend was Myrna Loy, and Myrna knew Bogart, and –'

'Carmody!' the Prize said urgently. 'Watch yourself! Have you ever heard of pseudo-acclimatization?'

'Don't be ridiculous,' Carmody said. 'I tell you, I know these people! I grew up here, and it was a damned good place to grow up in! People weren't just blobs like they are now; people really stood for something. People were *individuals* then, not crowds!'

'Are you quite sure of this? Your predator –'

'Rats, I don't want to hear any more about it,' Carmody said. 'Look! There's David Niven! His parents are English.'

'These people are coming towards you,' the Prize said.

'Well, sure they are,' Carmody said. 'They haven't seen me for a long time.'

He stood on the corner and his friends came down the pavement and the street, out of stores and shops. There were literally hundreds of them, all smiling, all old friends. He spotted Alan Ladd, Dorothy Lamour and Larry Buster Crabbe. And over there he saw Spencer Tracy, Lionel Barrymore, Freddy Bartholomew, John Wayne, Frances Farmer –

'There's something wrong with this,' the Prize said.

'Nothing's wrong,' Carmody insisted. His friends were all present, they were moving closer to him, holding out their hands, and he was happier than he had ever been since leaving his home. He was amazed that he could have forgotten how it had been. But he remembered now.

'Carmody!' the Prize shouted.

'What is it?'

'Is there always this music in your world?'

'What are you talking about?'

'I'm talking about the music,' the Prize said. 'Don't you hear it?'

Carmody noticed it for the first time. A symphony orchestra was playing, but he couldn't tell where it was coming from.

'How long has that been going on?'

'Ever since we got here,' the Prize told him. 'When you started down the street there was a soft thunder of drums. Then, when you passed the theatre, a lively air was played on a trumpet. This changed when you looked into the luncheonette, to a rather saccharine melody played by several hundred violins. Then –'

'That was background music,' Carmody said dully. 'This whole damned thing was scored, and I didn't even notice it.'

Franchot Tone reached out and touched his sleeve. Gary Cooper dropped a big hand on his shoulder. Laird Cregar gave him an affectionate bear hug. Shirley Temple seized his right foot. The others pressed closer, all still smiling.

'Seethwright!' Carmody shouted. 'For God's sake, Seethwright!'

After that, things happened a little too fast for his comprehension.

Part Five

The Return to Earth

Chapter 28

Carmody was in New York City, on Riverside Drive and Ninety-ninth Street. To the west, above the Jersey shore, the sun was dropping down behind Horizon House, and, to the right, the Spry sign had come on in all its glory. The trees of Riverside Park, clad in green and soot, rustled faintly in the exhaust fumes from the West Side Drive. Around him he could hear the screams of frustrated, highly strung children, punctuated by an occasional bellow from their equally frustrated and highly strung parents.

'Is this your home?' asked the Prize.

Carmody looked down and saw that the Prize had metamorphosed again, appearing now as a Dick Tracy watch with hidden stereo speaker.

'It looks like it,' Carmody said.

'Seems like rather an interesting spot,' the Prize said. 'Lively. I like that.'

'Yeah,' Carmody said reluctantly, not at all sure how he felt about his home.

He began to walk uptown. The lights had come on in Riverside Park. Mothers with baby carriages were leaving, and soon the park would be left alone to police cars and muggers. All around him the smog rolled in on little cat feet. Buildings could be glimpsed through it like giants who had lost their way. To either side, the sewers ran merrily into the Hudson, while at the same time the Hudson ran merrily into the sewers.

'Hey, Carmody!'

Carmody stopped and turned. A man was walking briskly towards him. The man wore a business suit, sneakers, a bowler, and a white canvas ascot. Carmody recognized him as George Marundi, an indigent artist of his acquaintance.

'Hey, man,' said Marundi, coming up and shaking hands.

'Hey, hey,' said Carmody, smiling like an accomplice.

'Well, man, how you *been*?' Marundi asked.

'Oh, you know,' Carmody said.

'Indeed, do I *not* know!' Marundi said. 'Helen's been asking about you.'

'That a fact?' Carmody said.

'Most assuredly. Dicky Tait's throwing a party next Saturday. You wanna come?'

'Sure,' Carmody said. 'How is Tait?'

'Well, man, you know.'

'Sure, I know,' Carmody said, in a tone of deep compassion. 'Still, eh?'

'What would you expect?' Marundi asked.

Carmody shrugged.

'Isn't anyone going to introduce me?' the Prize asked.

'Shut up!' Carmody said.

'Hey, man, what's that you got there?' Marundi bent down and peered at Carmody's wrist. 'Little tape recorder, huh? That's the greatest, baby, the greatest. You got it programmed?'

'I am not programmed,' the Prize said. 'I am autonomous.'

'Hey, that's beautiful!' Marundi said. 'I mean, it really is. Hey there, Mickey Mouse, what else you got to say?'

'Go screw yourself,' the Prize said.

'Stop it!' Carmody whispered urgently,

'Well now,' Marundi said, grinning, 'little fellow's got a lot of spunk, eh, Carmie?'

'That he has,' Carmody said.

'Where'd you get it?'

'I got it – well, I got it while I was away.'

'You've been away? I guess that's why I haven't seen you around for these last several months.'

'That must be it,' Carmody said.

'Where away have you been?' Marundi asked.

It was on the tip of Carmody's tongue to say that he had been in Miami. But instead he was inspired to say, 'I have been out in the Universe, the Cosmos itself, wherein I have passed through certain selected short subjects which shall henceforward be known as reality.'

Marundi nodded with understanding. 'You been on a Trip, yes, man?'

'Indeed I have.'

'And on that Trip you have perceived the molecular all-in-oneness of all things and have listened to the energies of your body, *nicht wahr?*'

'Not exactly,' Carmody said. 'Upon my particular Trip, I observed most particularly the discretionary energies of other creations and went beyond the personal-molecular into the external-atomic. That is to say, my Trip convinced me of the reality, to say nothing of the existence, of creatures other than myself.'

'That sounds like powerful acid,' Marundi said. 'Where might it be obtained?'

'The Acid of Experience is distilled from the dull weed of Practice,' Carmody said. 'Objective existence is desired by many but obtained by few.'

'You won't talk, huh?' Marundi said. 'Never mind, baby, any Trip you can make I can make better.'

'I doubt that.'

'I doubt not that you doubt that. But never mind. Are you coming to the Opening?'

'What Opening?'

Marundi looked at him with amazement. 'Man, you have not only been away, you have been out of touch besides. Today is the opening of what is past a doubt the most important art exhibition of our times and perhaps of any times.'

'What is this paragon of aesthetics?' Carmody asked.

'I am going there,' Marundi said. 'Accompany me.'

Despite the mumblings of the Prize, Carmody fell into step beside his friend. They walked uptown, and Marundi told the latest gossip: how the House Un-American Activities Committee had been found guilty of Un-Americanism but had got off with a suspended sentence; the success of Pepperidge Farm's new Freez-a-Man Plan; how five US Air Cavalry divisions had yesterday succeeded in killing five Vietcong guerrillas; how NBC-TV had begun a wildly successful new series entitled *Adventures in Laissez-Faire Capitalism*. And he also learned that General Motors, in a gesture of unprecendented patriotism, had sent a regiment of clerical volunteers led by a vice-president to Xien Ka near the Cambodian border.

Thus they conversed, and at length they came to 106th Street, where several buildings had been razed and a new structure erected to stand in their stead. This structure appeared to be a castle, but such a one as Carmody had never before seen. And he addressed his companion, the high-spirited Marundi, asking for an explanation.

'This massy building that you see before you,' Marundi said, 'was designed by the architect Delvanuey, who also planned Death Trap 66, the famous New York toll road which no one has succeeded in driving from start to finish without accident. This same Delvanuey, you may recall, drew up the plans for Flash-Point Towers, Chicago's newest slum, the only slum in the world in which form follows function; that is to say, the first slum which is proudly and avowedly designed *as* a slum, and which has been certified "unrenewable" by The President's Commission on the Perpetration of Fine Arts in Urbanamerica.'

'That is a singular accomplishment,' Carmody said. 'What does he call this particular structure?'

'This is his opus magnus,' Marundi said. 'This, my friend, is The Castle of Garbage.'

The roadway to the Castle, Carmody perceived, was cunningly constructed of egg shells, orange peels, avocado stones and clam shells. It led to a great doorway whose two sides were made of rusty bedsprings. Above the gate, in letters formed by varnished fishheads, was the motto: 'Wastefulness in the defence of luxury is no vice; moderation in the dissemination of excess is no virtue.'

They entered and walked through hallways of pressed cardboard, coming at last to an open courtyard in which a fountain of napalm blazed merrily away. They went past it into a room made of aluminium, steel, polyethylene, formica, styrene, bakelite, concrete, simulated walnut, acrilan and vinyl. Beyond that, other corridors branched out.

'Do you like it?' Marundi asked.

'I don't know yet,' Carmody said. 'What on earth is it?'

'It is a museum,' Marundi told him. 'It is the first museum of human waste.'

'I see,' Carmody said. 'How has it been received?'

'With great enthusiasm, to my amazement. I mean, we artists and intellectuals knew it was good, but we didn't think the public at large would catch on so fast. But they have. In this regard they have displayed innate good taste and have recognized this is the only true art of our times.'

'Do they? I, personally, find all of this a little hard to take.'

Marundi looked at him with sorrow. 'I had not thought that you of all people would be an aesthetic reactionary. What would you like? Greek statuary or Byzantine icons, perhaps?'

'Certainly not. But why this?'

'Because this, Carmody, is the real present, upon which true art must be constructed. We consume, therefore we are! But men have been unwilling to face this vital fact. They have turned away from Garbage, that irreducible residue of our pleasures. Yet consider – what is waste? Is it not a memorial to our needs? Waste not, want not: this was the ancient counsel of anal anxiety. But now the false axiom has been changed. Why talk about waste? Indeed! Why talk about sex, or virtue, or any other important thing?'

'It sounds reasonable when you put it that way,' Carmody said. 'But still . . .'

'Come with me, observe, learn,' Marundi said. 'The concept grows on you, very much like waste itself.'

They walked into the Extraneous Noises Room. Here Carmody listened to the sound of a continually flushing toilet, the musical pageant of traffic noises, the thrilling screech of an accident, the deep-throated roar of a mob. Mingled with this were Retrospective Sounds: the burr of a piston aircraft, the chatter of a riveting gun, the strong thud of a jackhammer. Past that was the Sonic Boom Room, which Carmody hastily backed out of.

'Quite right,' Marundi said. 'It *is* dangerous. But a lot of people come here, and some stay in this room for five or six hours.'

'Huh,' said Carmody.

'Perhaps,' Marundi said. 'Now, right over here is the keynote sound of our exhibition: the beloved bellow of a rubbish truck chewing up rubbish. Nice, eh? And right through here is an exhibition of empty pint wine bottles. Over there is a replica of a subway. It is built to convey every lurch, and its aerial environment is smoke-conditioned by Westinghouse.'

'What's that shouting?' Carmody asked.

'A tape of heroic voices,' Marundi said. 'That first one is Ed Brun, all-pro quarterback for the Green Bay Packers.

The next, a high-pitched whine, is a sound-portrait of New York's most recent mayor. And after that –'

'Let's go on,' Carmody said.

'Certainly. To the right is the Graffiti wing. To the left is an exact replica of an old-law tenement (a spurious bit of romanticism, to my way of thinking). Straight ahead you can see our collection of television antennas. This one is a British model, circa 1960. Note the severity, the restraint. Compare it to that 1959 Cambodian job. Do you see the luxuriant flowing of lines on the Oriental model? That is popular art expressing itself in a viable form.'

Marundi turned to Carmody and said earnestly, 'See and believe, my friend. This is the wave of the future. Once upon a time men resisted the implications of actuality. That day is gone. We know now that art is the thing itself together with its extensions into superfluity. Not pop art, I hasten to say, which sneers and exaggerates. This is *popular* art, which simply exists. This is the age in which we unconditionally accept the unacceptable, and thus proclaim the naturalness of our artificiality.'

'I don't like it!' Carmody said. 'Seethwright!'

'What are you shouting for?' Marundi asked him.

'Seethwright! Seethwright! Get me the hell out of here!'

'He's flipped,' Marundi said. 'Is there a doctor in the house?'

Immediately a short swarthy man in a one-piece jumpsuit appeared. The man was carrying a little black bag with a silver plaque on it, upon which was written, 'Little Black Bag.'

'I am a physician,' the physician said. 'Let me see him.'

'Seethwright! Where in hell are you?'

'Hmmmmmm, I see,' the doctor said. 'This man shows every sign of acute hallucinatory deprivation. Hmm. Yes, I palpate the head and find a hard massy growth. That much is normal. But going beyond that . . . hmm, amazing. The poor man is literally starved for illusion.'

'Doc, can you help him?' Marundi asked.

'You called me just in time,' the doctor said. 'The condition is reversible. I have here the divine panacea.'

'Seethwright!'

The doctor drew a case out of his Little Black Bag and fitted together a glittering hypodermic. 'This is the standard booster,' he said to Carmody. 'Nothing to worry about, it wouldn't hurt a child. It contains a highly pleasing mixture of LSD, barbiturates, amphetamines, tranquillizers, psychic lifts, mood stimulators, and various other good things. And just a touch of arsenic to make your hair glossy. Hold still now . . .'

'Damn you, Seethwright! Get me out of this!'

'It only hurts while the pain is present,' the doctor assured him, poised the hypodermic and thrust home.

At the same moment, or nearly the same moment, Carmody disappeared.

There was consternation and confusion in the Castle, which was not resolved until everyone had fixed. Then it was passed-over with Olympian calm. As for Carmody, a priest intoned the words: 'Superfluous man, goest thou now to that great realm, of the Extraneous in the sky, where there is place for all unnecessary things.'

But Carmody himself, propelled by the faithful Seeth-wright, plunged onward through the endless worlds. He moved in a direction best characterized as 'down,' through the myriad potentialities of Earth, and into the clustered improbabilities, and finally into the serried ranges of the constructed impossibilities.

The Prize chided him, saying, 'That was your own world that you abandoned, Carmody! Are you aware of that?'

'Yes, I am aware of it,' Carmody said.

'And now there can be no return.'

'I am aware of that, too.'

'I suppose you thought you'd find some gaudy utopia in the worlds ahead?' the Prize said, with a marked sneer.

'No, not exactly.'

'What then?'

Carmody shook his head and refused to answer.

'Whatever it was, you can forget about it,' the Prize said bitterly. 'Your predator is close behind you and will infallibly be your death.'

'I don't doubt it,' Carmody said, in a moment of strange calm. 'But in terms of long-range planning, I never did expect to get out of this Universe alive.'

'That is meaningless,' the Prize said. 'The fact is, you have lost everything.'

'I don't agree,' Carmody said. 'Permit me to point out that I am presently still alive.'

'Agreed. But only for the moment.'

'I have always been alive only for the moment,' Carmody said. 'I could never count on more. It was my error to expect more. That holds true, I believe, for all of my possible and potential circumstances.'

'Then what do you hope to achieve with your moment?'

'Nothing,' Carmody said. 'Everything.'

'I don't understand you any longer,' the Prize said. 'Something about you has changed, Carmody. What is it?'

'A minor thing,' Carmody told him. 'I have simply given up a longevity which I never possessed anyhow. I have turned away from the con game which the Gods run in their heavenly sideshow. I no longer care under which shell the pea of immortality might be found. I don't need it. I have my moment, which is quite enough.'

'Saint Carmody!' the Prize said, in tones of deepest sarcasm. 'No more than a shadow's breadth separates you and death! What will you do now with your pitiable moment?'

'I shall continue to live it,' Carmody said. 'That is what moments are for.'